ABSINTHE & ARSENIC

ABSINTHE & ARSENIC
RAVEN DANE

Published in the UK by Telos Moonrise
(an imprint of Telos Publishing)
17 Pendre Avenue, Prestatyn, Denbighshire, LL19 9SH

Absinthe & Arsenic © 2013 Raven Dane
Foreword © 2013 Raven Dane
Cover Design by David J Howe

ISBN: 978-1-84583-858-4 (Paperback)

British Library Cataloguing in Publication Data. A catalogue record for this book is available from the British Library.

CONTENTS

FOREWORD

Long before I became obsessed with all things steampunk, I loved ghost stories, and in particular, Victorian spooky tales. I avidly read stories by Wilkie Collins and M R James as a teenager and loved to be terrified by the film and television adaptations of their work. One in particular – the BBC's adaptation of *The Ash-Tree* by M R James – still haunts my nightmares decades later!

This collection is my homage to this wonderful genre, celebrating a time of gaslight and fog, Penny Dreadfuls, the rattle of Hansom cabs along cobbled streets and the rustle of silk bustles in the deadly haze of opium dens.

Most of the stories in this collection were written especially for the book. Exceptions include 'The Attic Nursery', which was my first ever attempt at a ghost story from the dawn of my writing career, and an excerpt from my award winning steampunk novel, *Cyrus Darian and the Technomicron*.

'In *Insomnium Veritas*' was written as a personal challenge to create a story infused with all the themes of classic gothic literature: gloomy castles, obsession, deep shadows, doomed love and a palpable sense of the macabre. It is not my usual writing style but I hope I rose to the challenge.

'A Taste of Almonds' was chosen from hundreds of submissions to be part of the first Christmas spooky annual from Spectral Press called *The 13 Ghosts of Christmas*. Published in December 2012 to great critical acclaim, this story was singled out many times as one of the highlights of the book, which was both a personal delight and deep honour for me.

I hope you enjoy reading this selection of my stories as much as I enjoyed writing them.

Raven Dane
February 2013

THE 10.15 TO LEALHOLM

North Yorkshire, 1877

The Journal of Edwin Hazeldine Esquire.

I write this account of my horrible experience that began on the 10.15 to Lealholm for myself, as if transcribing the occurrence will somehow lesson the frightful toll it has had on my person. I do not expect anyone else to read it or to believe a word of my encounter. Nor do I longer care. I know what happened.

Three days ago, I found myself journeying to visit my elder brother who lived on a godforsaken remote farm on the North Yorkshire moors. He had previously sent me a peculiar missive, almost unreadable in its ramblings, and I was certain Gregory had succumbed to some sort of disorder of the mind. Being both close in the past and always most fond of my sibling, I hurried to investigate his state of health and to seek professional help for him if needed. Cost was not a problem, for my investments in the City had yielded excellent returns and I enjoyed a life of comfort and leisure from my home in Kensington, with no wife or family to add responsibility.

All this seemed a lifetime away from the bleak and

windswept platform I found myself impatiently pacing, in Middlesbrough, waiting for the one train that would cross the moors and get me that bit closer to Four Winds House and my brother. I had acted on impulse on receiving the missive from my brother and had not planned my journey in advance. It was unlikely that a pony and carriage would be available to hire at this time of the night on my arrival, nor could I contemplate a four mile hike across the dangerous moors by night. My only hope was to find an inn with a room in Lealholm and continue to Gregory's remote home on the morning.

At the correct time by my pocket watch, a small locomotive chugged into the station and paused, the boiler groaning and wheezing like an ageing and impatient dragon. There were three carriages, mostly empty, one for each class. I found a seat in first class and prepared for the slow haul over the moors, so beautiful in their bleak majesty by day, nothing but miles of darkness by the cloak of night. I was alone, which suited me well, being in no mood for casual conversation with strangers with my anxiety over my brother at the forefront of my mind. Though of course, had there been another voyager, I would have been civil and joined in any discourse.

Within an hour, the long day's travelling from London began to take its toll, my eyelids became lead-weighted, my head jerking as I fought the onset of sleep. I must have lost the unequal battle, succumbing to a strange dream of being on a horse-drawn omnibus that had become unattached to its team and was careering out of control. A sudden jolt of the train brought me back into reality. I was no longer alone.

Despite the many empty seats, a new passenger had the bad manners to sit directly opposite me. The style and poor quality of his torn and soaking wet clothing suggested he was in the wrong carriage. The man was thick-set and burly with a disagreeable countenance beneath a crushed and dirty brown bowler. His boots were mud-caked, the soles ragged and coming detached. I did what any English gentleman would in these awkward circumstances and reached for my copy of the *Observer*, feigning intense interest in the newspaper despite having read it already from cover to cover during my journey – twice.

For some time there was nothing but an uneasy silence above the rattle and rhythm of the train and the man's hoarse breathing. I began to feel churlish; clearly he was unwell. As his respiration became more laboured, I lowered my newspaper to find him staring at me with wide, reddened and unblinking eyes. His face was pale yet flushed with rivulets of sweat, and his body shook as if in the first stage of a seizure.

'My poor fellow,' I murmured, 'you are in a bad way … Is there anything I can do to help you? Fetch some water, perhaps?'

His answer was a deep, animal-like groan, more of anger than pain, and my unease veered into a curious, primal fear and thoughts of escape. I glanced back to the adjoining second class carriage but could see no sign of any passengers. I was certain that at least six had alighted at Middlesbrough. But now the carriage was empty. With the third class compartment out of my range of vision, I appeared to be alone apart from my unwelcome fellow traveller.

With no other choice, I returned to my newspaper, believing moving to another seat might trigger an angry response from the unpleasant and possibly unhinged stranger. I did not relax my guard but the man remained seated, his breathing gradually becoming less laboured until it quietened to an eerie silence. Had he died, sitting upright in his seat? By now I was too alarmed to dare to look and began to pray the train would quickly reach another moorland station and allow me to escape.

Another ten minutes or so passed in silence with no movement from my unwanted fellow traveller. It seemed an eternity to me. My heart missed more than one beat as he groaned, a sound now deepened to a bestial snarl. I threw down my useless paper shield to discover his pallor becoming tinged with a horrible shade of green, his glaring eyes now filled with an insane fury. A hideous drool of reeking saliva ran from blackened lips. The passenger was not ill; he had become a monster before my horrified eyes. I leapt to my feet, desperate for a means of defence and escape. The speed of the train remained too great to leap from the carriage, but it was still an option, the prospect of broken bones and concussion a fair price to pay to be away from this nightmare.

Struggling to arise from his seat, the passenger was poorly co-ordinated, a shambling mound of flesh, one I was able to sidestep with ease. Holding my cane like a sword, I stood my ground against this foe of unknown strength and purpose. My posture of defence made no difference to the fellow's deranged aggression, only his difficulty in perambulation preventing me from being overpowered.

Hell itself descended in a deafening explosion, the carriage appeared to rise high in the air then crash down to earth in a tortured scream of rent metal, an upheaval that sent both me and my foe tumbling helpless as rag dolls hurled by a monstrous child. Buffeted and badly bruised, I fell awkwardly beneath the seats and lay there dazed, shocked but alive. God must have wanted me to live, because that location saved me from the worst carnage of the derailed carriage as it collapsed in a frenzy of spars of jagged wood and torn metal. I could not see the other passenger but had no interest in his fate. In fact I hoped he was buried beneath the ruin of the carriage, for there was no doubt he meant to kill me with his bare hands.

I have no concept of how long I remained wedged beneath the seat, trapped by the piles of broken carriage. Once the metallic groans of the train in its death throes had settled, the silence gave me no hope of rescue. That no-one else on the train was screaming or moaning in pain told volumes; that by some miracle, I was alone in surviving the crash. The remoteness and sparse population of the moors also meant no hope of a speedy rescue, and as I smelled a choking smoke coming from the stricken locomotive and the crackle of nearing flames, I had no choice but to extricate myself from this dire predicament.

The rapid approach of the inferno gave me added strength. Fighting the natural urge to panic, I forced myself from under the debris, ignoring further bruises and a nasty, deep gash to my temple from a razor sharp piece of metal. As the carriage had fallen on its side, my convoluted and exhausting escape route was through the broken window above my head. Already dense, oily black smoke from the all-devouring fire had billowed into my carriage. I refused to succumb to this next catastrophe and, climbing through the ruins, hauled myself out of the window, gaining further injury from the shards of broken glass.

The descent from the upended carriage onto the wreckage-strewn surrounds became a leap of faith, trusting my fear and that my exertion-weakened legs would not buckle as I landed on burning grass and heather. I clambered up the steep embankment, grabbing handfuls of long, tough grass for purchase, and bolted towards the open moor.

Never had fresh air been sweeter as I breathed in deep lungfuls, my head spinning as if drunk on it. Believing myself safe from the disaster, I glanced back to see a vision of Hell itself. What caused the derailment was not apparent. The locomotive was tipped to one side while the first and second class carriages were on their sides and now fully ablaze. Only the third class remained on the rails in a crooked manner but there was no sign of a living being emerging from the mercifully flame-free carriage. I searched my soul for any residual heroism, in particular in view of my miraculous salvation, and realised I could not stumble away from the disaster without checking for any unfortunates in need of rescue.

As I began to walk back down towards the remaining carriage, I paused at a sign of movement. Three figures fell out of the still-functioning carriage doors and landed on their knees on the trackside. A man and two women. My relief at their survival turned to horror as they began to move with the same disjointed, shuffling gait as my earlier protagonist. The fiery light from the blazing train illuminated their wild, staring eyes, glassy and unfocused as if they were dead, their mouths stained and dripping with fresh blood and strips of gore-stained pale flesh. Whatever these monstrous creatures were, all humanity was now lost.

My already weakened legs failed me, and I fell, weeping with terror, onto the damp grass. Unable to look away, I found my gaze drawn to the blazing first class carriage as a smoking shape appeared from the same broken window that had afforded me an escape route. My mouth opened in a silent scream as my foe descended to join the other monsters. His coat smouldered and he was equally oblivious to the shaft of wood piercing his chest and emerging from his back. Frozen with revulsion, I watched as he blundered to the others of his monstrous kind. There was no recognition or visible communication between the figures but as one they turned, voracious eyes fixing on mine.

I needed no spurring on to flee for my life. Primal instinct galvanised my limbs, for I was prey. The pale and bloodied flesh caught in my pursuers' teeth was obviously that of the other passengers. With no plan or destination, I gathered the last of my wits and strength and hurled myself across the open moor, not caring whence I ran as long as it was far away. My hope for survival lay in my speed and agility even across the treacherous terrain as compared to their awkward and disjointed shuffle. Even the prospect of falling into a deep morass and drowning seemed preferable to being torn apart and devoured alive.

Darkness hampered my every stride. The stars were cloaked in low cloud, gravid with the threat of heavy rain. The uneven and heather-strewn ground tripped me many times but even with the risk of a turned or broken ankle I could not slow down – dared not slow down – memory of the murderous glares from those creatures hastening my every stride.

I ran until I could only stumble, lungs seared with pain, legs weak. Then, when I could no longer stumble, I crawled on my hands and knees, helpless as an infant but refusing to stop. Of course my body could not take such abuse indefinitely and I sought refuge in the paltry shelter of a dip in the landscape behind a hillock. I had no idea how long I remained there as my body attempted to recover, gasping for breath and shivering with cold and fear. I had no water though the surroundings were dank and I had splashed through many brackish pools. The low clouds gave up their uneven struggle to carry their heavy burden and I lifted my face to the sky, drinking in as much precious rainwater as I could. When the rain had finished, mercifully the sky cleared with the promise of daybreak spearing the horizon. I could not bear to linger any longer and with difficulty struggled to my feet and headed towards the dawn.

What a sight I must have presented to any fellow on my blundering path, filthy, soaked to the skin, my hands and face torn by brambles and bruised by many falls. Daylight brought me hope as I saw that a farmhouse stood within stumbling distance. Gathering the last fragments of my depleted strength, I aimed for that dwelling with the fervour of a man stranded in a desert crawling to an oasis.

The stillness of the farm was increasingly curious the closer I got to the stalwart stone buildings. Daybreak should have been a busy, noisy time with cattle demanding milking, dogs barking, other stock calling for feeding, but not even a lone chicken scratched among the cobbles. No lights shone from the farmhouse window, and the place appeared abandoned. It was still much needed shelter, so approaching with caution I entered the main yard in front.

I caught a streak of blue, grey and white bound before me: a working collie bitch, hackles raised, teeth bared into threatening fangs, a deep growl of warning building up in her throat. But her demeanour changed as she caught my scent, and she dropped down to the cobbles into a fawning crawl, whimpering with need. I wondered how long the poor creature had been abandoned to fend for herself.

'Steady lass,' I crooned, caressing her filthy, soaking merle coat and moved by the innocent joy in her blue eyes. On closer inspection, I could see the collie was in a bad way, thin and with signs of being in a fight, with gashes caked over with dried blood. The front door of the house was closed but not locked and, though not expecting a reply, I called out for the farmer as I stepped into the hall. My voice echoed unanswered and though it went against all good manners and the behaviour expected of a civilised Englishman, I sought out the kitchen.

There had been no activity here for some time. The range was stone cold and the rancid stench from a milk pitcher by the sink was stomach-churning. Closer inspection of the cupboards rewarded me with a good ham, some cheese and a tin of sweet biscuits. Odd fare, but to the dog and me, it was sent directly from Paradise. Drawing fresh water from the indoor pump, I also found some dry kindling for the range and within the hour I was clean and refreshed with black tea. With the collie snuggled close, I must have dozed off, then fallen into a deep, coma-like sleep, because when I finally stirred it was once more dark.

Some old survival instinct warned me not to create any light: on these flat moors even a single oil lamp could shine out like a beacon, attracting not only the benign but also those monstrous, degraded beings with the outer shell of a human being. My long rest in this desolate house had given my possible pursuers an advantage. Only an optimism born of fear and desperation would lead to the conclusion that they had lost interest in my living flesh or had fallen victim to the many treacherous quagmires on the moor. I needed to move on, though I would no longer be alone. Bess, as I called the collie, would be at my side as companion and a sharp nose for impending danger.

I fell into another deep, unwanted sleep, slumped over the kitchen table, and awoke as the first wan, red-tinged light of dawn breached the horizon. My terror-filled flight had numbed my senses on arrival at the farmhouse. Now rested, I was more aware of my surroundings, and realisation grew that this was the site of a slaughter. Dried blood and gore stains started in the hall and trailed from the upper floor, the sickly stench of putrefaction wafted down, and I knew whoever once dwelled in this stalwart home was long dead. I could not bear to see the carnage. What use could I be to the victims? The last traces of civilised behaviour were put to one side as I helped myself to anything in the kitchen and downstairs that could be of use.

The discovery of a framed map in the hall yielded me a direction … Travel due north and I would be close to my brother's home. I smashed the glass and frame holding the map, which I folded and placed in the breast pocket of my purloined jacket, without a twinge of guilt over my vandalism. I strode out, Bess at my heels and a knapsack packed full of provisions on my back. I wore more treasure in the form of a waxed cape coat and deerstalker hat to keep out the wind and rain that was surely threatened by the red sky. In my hand was a stout walking stick to ease my passage across the rough moors. Alas I could find no firearms; no doubt these were in the hands of the corpses on the upper floor. A less squeamish man would have prised them from their stiffened grasps, but I could not even summon the courage to look.

Then came another gift from the unfortunate farmer. In an orchard paddock grazed a sturdy moorland cob, a Sales Galloway by his colour and confirmation. He had been kept in by a high, old stone walling. There was a stream of spring water running through the little field and plenty of grass, so the animal had not suffered from his master's terrible demise. He came readily to call and, though I was loathe to hang around this place of death, my escape would be so much swifter with a pony and farm cart.

I struggled not to yield to natural panic as my fear numbed-fingers struggled with the harness straps, but with the black cob's calm patience helping, somehow I managed to secure them. With Bess beside me on the driving seat, I was soon trotting up a well-worn track.

My spirits were at last raised beyond complete despair, helped by being fed, well rested and driving a happy and willing cob across the moors in daylight. For the first time since fleeing the wreck of the 10.15 to Lealholm, I was warm and dry and no longer alone thanks to my new canine friend who sat beside me, her intelligent face wreathed in the canine equivalent of a broad smile.

The pony's brisk pace ate up the miles and, with Lealholm Bridge in sight, I considered recuperating at The Board Inn, a well-appointed 18th Century coaching tavern. I also needed to discover if others had encountered the cannibalistic monsters and if the militia had been summoned to engage them. I breached a hilltop and reined in the cob to a halt. I knew from past visits that the village lay nestled in a heather-strewn moorland valley, snug with picturesque stone buildings and a winding river. But now an appalling scene lay below my horrified gaze. Most of Lealholm was ablaze, its streets strewn with debris and what appeared to be dead bodies. My attention turned to what I hoped was a survivor approaching from the stricken village, someone who needed my aid and could tell me what had happened, but as he neared the cart, his shuffling, lurching gait, gore-stained clothing and glaring inhuman eyes were those of another monster.

The startled cob needed no urging as I wheeled him around. He spun the cart on a perilously tight circle and galloped away from Lealholm and the horrible thing on the road. The likelihood of finding my brother alive was fading but what else could I do? Now his ramblings to me in his last letter made sense. Gregory had seen these hideous transformations and gruesome deaths. Maybe this knowledge had spurred him on to protect himself in his home; he was a brave and resourceful man. Armed only with this ember of hope, I had no choice but to seek out another route across the moors, which would unfortunately be one less well-paved and serviceable.

Such was the steep and winding nature of these other tracks, it was not until late afternoon that the weary cob finally approached the drive to my brother's home. I reined him in, unwilling to approach straight up to the doorway without knowing Gregory's situation. All seemed peaceful. On the surrounding hillsides, my brother's prized herd of shaggy Wensleydale sheep grazed unconcerned amongst the gorse and heather. Though the day was drawing in, I could make out no light from the farmhouse or smoke rising from any of the many chimneys of his substantial home. I did not know how to proceed, though with the cob spent and no welcome back in Lealholm except from voracious cannibals, I had no backup plan.

An upstairs window opened, and even in the dimming light I could make out the metal gleam of a rifle barrel. A familiar voice barked down at me.

'Have you been bitten?'

I stood up in the cart and waved back at my brother, relief spilling into unashamed tears down my cheeks. 'No Greg, I am unharmed, just exhausted and very afraid.'

'Wait there.'

The hostile tone in his voice spoke of fear, not of any enmity between us, and I waited patiently while he scrutinised my face and demeanour through a high powered telescope.

'Are you alone?'

'Just me, a collie dog and the Galloway for company.'

'Has it been bitten?' he continued to my alarm. I had not considered Bess to be a threat. I checked over her wounds again with meticulous care. All her slight injuries were bramble scratches. I could not see anything even vaguely resembling a bite mark.

'She is clear, Greg. Do you want me to check the cob?'

'No need. Horses and other grazing beasts are not carriers. Drive around to the stable yard but be on your guard. I had to sleep for a few hours and they may have returned.'

With this worrying news, I clicked the tired cob into one last trot on our journey. Anticipating a warm stable and hay, he pricked his ears forward and brought me quickly into the stable yard. Armed with two rifles and a couple of fearsome English mastiffs that I recognised as his pets, Hengist and Horsa, my brother helped unhitch the cob and get him settled in another small paddock.

'Safer for the pony than a stable,' my brother pointed out, his mouth set in a grim line, his eyes restless, checking for danger. 'They only devour human flesh but love to kill anything for the sake of it. Bastards.'

'What are they?' I asked, desperate for an answer.

'Could be you or me, all it takes is a bite from one of them through to the blood,' Gregory replied, practically dragging me into the house, which I discovered resembled a fortress with all the downstairs windows and all but one side door boarded up with heavy planks. Once we were all inside, he turned and nailed that door up too.

'They are slow, stupid but strong and determined.'

Gregory showed me the outside of one of the planks, gouged with hundreds of scratches.

'From their finger nails …'

Overcome by horror, I must have fainted, for when I became aware again, I was with Gregory and the dogs in an upstairs room, which was prepared for a long siege. My brother had collected barrels of water, boxes of tinned and dried food and a collection of shotguns with ammunition. He had placed an armchair by the window and by the blankets beside it. This was where Gregory spent his days and nights, in constant vigilance. It showed on his haggard, unshaven face, and his eyes had an unhealthy glitter, sunk deep into dark shadows.

'You need to rest, Greg. I am here now; we can take turns to keep watch.'

He nodded and gave a soul deep sigh. 'Thank you, Eddie. I have kept vigil for over a week now. I am so tired. So very tired.'

As he slipped straight away into a deep sleep in the same armchair by the window, I must admit to a curious sense of relief. Despite the catastrophic and bizarre circumstances of our reunion, my brother was not insane. No dreadful malady had robbed him of his senses. At least, not yet. Being under siege by hideous monsters for any length of time could change all that for both of us.

We have been together under siege in the farmhouse for three weeks now. Water is not a problem, with a deep bore hole well set within the dwelling, and we have a well-stocked dry wood supply. Rationing the food supply has become vital, and we are always hungry. Occasionally a pheasant or one of the farm's chickens wanders into the yard. Greg shot them at first, bringing a welcome supply of fresh meat, but the sound of gunfire attracted our enemies. Within hours of potting some fowl, a shambling gang of sub-humans attempted to breach our defences. Their form had deteriorated since my first sighting of other such creatures at the train crash. Their bodies were bloated and rotting, exposing bone where the flesh had fallen away. It was then I realised the full horror of what we were facing … These things were animated corpses, dead yet still moving.

What motivated them to continue in this mockery of life was unknown, but my brother and I were certain of one thing. They craved living human flesh, maybe to sustain their unnatural existence or perhaps in response to some primal urge to try to reactivate their own dead, rotting flesh with the spirit of the still-living. Despite the horror of their appearance and the danger they presented, such deterioration gave us hope. Surely eventually full decomposition would bring an end to their existence?

Any chance of an easier escape was lost when the Galloway had enough of the small paddock and the danger from the creatures. Sensibly it leapt the stone wall and returned to living wild on the moors like its ancestors, but we had lost our transport ... such an advantage over fleeing on foot.

Tonight, we sit in darkness, not wanting any oil lamp or hearth fire to act as a beacon and attract the monsters that may still be out there. A fiery glow on the far horizon catches Greg's attention, a ruddy, ugly light that does not auger well. The baleful light remains there undiminished for hours. Greg tells me it could be the coastal town of Whitby. It must be engulfed by a terrible inferno and any hope of finding safety there has gone.

We will wait as long as we can, in the apparent safety of the farmhouse fortress. We cannot give up hope that Her Majesty's armed forces will rid us of this Godless scourge or that the vile foe will all rot away to self-defeat.

Our food is virtually gone and we can endure no more of this siege despite the harsh weather conditions that have befallen us. This morning Greg and I, with our loyal dogs, will venture forth in search of the living. We have packed enough supplies for a few days, loading them on a makeshift sled, and have the shotguns and a good supply of ammunition. The blizzard that raged for several days has gone, and sunlight sparkles on thick virgin snow, giving the impression of a world of innocence, that I know is nothing but an illusion. Will we find safe sanctuary or a world ending in carnage and fear?

I will leave this journal behind as a record of what has happened here on the Yorkshire Moors.

May God protect and guide us.

And you …

Edwin Hazeldine Esquire. January, 1877

ANNIE BY GASLIGHT

London, 1888

As always, their raucous laughter drew Annie to her bedroom window: a brash gaggle of local women, arms linked, stepping out for the night in their finery. They passed beneath the gaslight below her in their well-worn gowns, bustled skirts dragging along the dank, cobbled street.

Annie loved to sit on the edge of her bed and gaze out of the window at bedtime. Below her, the narrow street stayed busy long after dark, illuminated by a circle cast by the green, eerie gaslight directly beneath her bedroom window. She was fascinated by this wonder, how its brightness stayed constant unlike the warmer but flickering and fragile lights of candles that lit her home after dark.

Her parents had not converted their small terraced home in Whitechapel to the new gas. Annie understood why, for even at eight years old, she was aware how hard her father and now her eldest brother worked to support their family. Annie had three sisters, two brothers, and another two siblings looking down from Heaven. A new baby slumbered in her mother's belly, though not for much longer. Papa worked long hours and came home well after dark in the winter. They simply could not afford to light their narrow little terrace home with gas.

Annie's fascination with the gas lamp first began when she stayed up late to wait for her father's safe return. He was an engineer, employed in the ambitious project to build an underground rail system beneath London's streets. It was dangerous, pioneering work and bad injuries or even fatalities were not uncommon among the workers.

Even after her father was crippled by a rock fall and was moved from the underground works to a lesser paid office position, Annie still kept up her habit of looking out of the bedroom window at night until her eyelids grew heavy and she finally snuggled beneath the bedclothes to join her sisters in the bed they shared, tightly packed under the covers like sardines in a tin.

By now she was familiar with many of the locals who passed beneath her, briefly caught in the flare of the gas lamp before returning to the darkness beyond its circle of light. Among them were noisy, cheerful gangs of Irish labourers on their way to the nearest pub to slake away a long day's hard work and the familiar quartet of streetwalkers, gossiping and giggling on their way to ply their tawdry trade. Annie did not yet know what that trade was but she loved the way the women did their best to look fashionable: a new, bright-coloured feather tucked into a battered old bonnet; a smear of rouge on their pale cheeks and lips. She heard their loud, brash attempt at gaiety, unaware it was fuelled by cheap gin and laudanum used in an attempt to stifle the danger and degradation of their lives. To the little girl, they seemed so carefree, so glamorous. They were a lively part of the teeming street life beneath her window.

But times changed. A spreading fear now seeped beneath every front door and through every window in the East End, infecting all within; a terror spread on the wind that was too great for Annie's mother to hide from her family. She became pale and gaunt, so frightened of the dark and shadows. The fear diminished her, turning her into a living ghost of her former confident self. Insisting on heavy iron bars on the downstairs windows and many new sturdy door locks, Annie's mother kept her children inside as soon as the day aged and darkened. Nothing would induce her to leave her home after dark, nor could she stop her anxious vigil until her husband and son were safely home from their toil.

Annie did not stop her nightly vigil by her window though, not even after the gossiping, happy quartet of streetwalkers became a frightened, scurrying group of three. Bad things were happening in Whitechapel and Annie no longer gazed at the light but peered into what lay beyond it. The still darkness was a veil hiding something, destroying all safety and security in her world, turning her mother and the mothers of her friends into fear-haunted wraiths.

The days turned, nights grew longer and the fearful streetwalkers ran beneath the lamp by Annie's window. The navvies still continued along their well-worn route to the nearest inns but there was no cheeriness in their gait, instead they strode along in a tight, protective pack, as alert as prey beasts.

Inevitably the change of season brought back to

the streets the scourge of a heavy, filthy fog, nicknamed the London Particular, turning day into a weak copy of night and night into a shroud. And still Annie kept her lonely vigil by the window after dark, watching the gaslight struggle to spread its wan beams through the swirling brown blanket that appeared to have a malign life of its own.

Few were foolish enough to venture far into the choking fog. It was a beast with no features, no limbs, and it engulfed the city with its sulphurous smoke-stained breath.

One night, as Annie turned her attention away from the weak circle of light and gazed into the depths of the fog, a shiver of movement caught her eye. A face? She fell back from the windowsill, the brief sighting enough to terrify her. The face was human in form but made from the fog, merging from it and disappearing back into the glowing darkness. She remembered it had no eyes, but two orbs of darker fog; the same formed a mouth open in a wide, silent scream.

Annie felt afraid. Her sobbing did not wake her siblings but alerted Albert, her oldest brother and confidant, as he passed by the half-open door.

He sat beside her on the edge of the bed and listened to her tale, placing a thin, comforting arm around her shoulders.

''Tis nuffink but the Particular playing tricks on yer, Annie,' he soothed. 'Everyone is well spooked at the moment.'

Albert shut himself up from elaborating why, remembering not to talk about the savage murders of local fallen women. Rumours were as common as pigeons, lurid and rife with talk of a knife-wielding maniac, possibly a toff, or a gang of cruel foreigners.

Even the old, wild stories of the demonic Spring Heeled Jack returning to frighten the neighbourhood. One eerie story was kept between the wives, sweethearts and widows of the railway labourers. It was a whispered secret of some frightful event in the tunnel beneath Whitechapel. An incident that was kept hushed up by the toffs because too much money and prestige were at stake to allow anything to halt the tunnelling.

Something long buried had been released. Something intangible yet utterly malign.

Albert had heard it from a girl he was sweet on, the daughter of a navvy. He never repeated the rumour, because he prayed it was just someone's runaway imagination sparked by the release of some trapped marsh gas.

Pushing aside these fanciful musings, he held on tightly to his sister in the darkness, feeling her tears soak his nightshirt. Such a tale was nonsense, had to be, and he would never scare Annie by telling her about it now.

'No good staring out the window, little Annie, a pea-souper will always make yer see fings that ain't there. Back to yer nice warm bed.'

Once she had settled, Albert waited until she slumbered peacefully next to her sisters then moved across to the window, ready to close the curtains. But not before he too gazed out at the gas lamp, drawn to what lay beyond.

Albert saw a ripple of movement in the fog, human shapes but too fast-moving and sinuous to be natural. One paused to glance up, a terror-filled face briefly made of shadow and fog, before dissolving back into the filthy, brown miasma. Stifling a horrified shriek, Albert pulled the curtains across, hard enough to risk tearing them off the rail. His whole body shivered with terror. With the room in complete darkness, he considered lighting the bedside candle, but chose to stumble his way out onto the landing and back to his own room. The darkness was preferable to dancing shadows on the walls. As he lay, shaking, in the shared bed, he fought to be strong. At 13 he was a man, after all. One who worked hard as a road-sweeper, earned his keep. It was as he told Annie, nothing but the fog playing tricks. He would accept no other explanation.

It was still dark when Albert got up and prepared to go to work, but the fog had gone, washed away by a steady downpour of cold rain. To his dismay, the eerie events of the past night lingered in his mind as he hurried to the depot, head down, cap pulled low over his eyes.

Annie and her sisters came down for breakfast before doing their daily chores. To her sadness, the atmosphere at home had worsened. Unable to hide the puffiness and streaks from tearful eyes, her mother had obviously been crying. With no explanation, Annie wondered, did her mother weep from sheer terror? Maybe the bad thing that was haunting the adults had struck again. Why wouldn't her mother tell her what was going on? It was more upsetting not to know. Her mother answered her unspoken question by hugging Annie as tightly as her pregnancy could allow.

'Do not fret, lass. You'll be all growed up soon enuf, time aplenty to worry about bad fings.'

The day settled into a normal routine, Annie sitting by her mother's side as soon as there was enough daylight to work by, learning to be a seamstress like her and helping the family coffers by doing simple repairs. The atmosphere would remain tense until her father and Albert returned home.

Eyes aching, fingers sore and numb, Annie was grateful for a break in her sewing when her mother, looking more pale-faced and fragile than ever, asked her to get her younger siblings their tea. The day had passed so swiftly, night had crept in unnoticed like an intruder. Annie lit the downstairs oil lamps and began cutting bread … not too thick slices, the loaf had to stretch to the whole family, with the largest portions kept aside for the working men of the household.

A shriek! Annie dropped the knife to discover her mother lying on the floor, clutching her belly. The baby was coming early and from her mother's fear-filled face, something was wrong. With no-one else to help, Annie did her best to make her comfortable and then, flinging on a shawl, ran to seek assistance from the neighbours.

The fog had returned with nightfall. It swallowed her up in a dank embrace from the moment she stepped outside but Annie had to force aside her fear. She ignored the stinging, foul air and ran to find help. There was none to be had. Fear had slammed shut all windows and locked all doors to her. It was as though the houses were stern faces and, as one, they closed their blind window eyes, ignoring her pleas, as curtains were pulled tight. She could not contemplate returning home without finding help. Babies were born and died, but the thought of losing her mother to Heaven and the angels was unbearable.

The Particular muffled her footsteps on the street as she made her way toward the home of Old Granny Bett, the woman who helped most of the neighbourhood's babies into the world ... and out of it, if need be. A no-nonsense, sinewy unofficial midwife of Romani blood. Annie reasoned the woman would be far too tough to be scared of the fog. What frightened the child now was the thought of losing her way; visibility close to the lamplights was poor, beyond them, impossible. And she was no longer alone.

Whatever followed behind her was not human. Nor was it the rhythmic metal-shod clop of a carriage horse. The footfall sounded like that of a horse but was heavy and erratic, with gaps in between as if something on two legs was jumping from one side of the street to the next. Annie screamed and began to run, no longer caring where she went. Her only thought was to escape from the entity. When she turned left down a street, she was certain that *it* did also. That it was giving chase.

Fighting for breath in the toxic air, Annie reached a gas light, clinging to it as if the wan circle of light could keep the bad thing pursuing her at bay. Around her the fog seemed to thicken even more, coalescing into vaguely human forms. Faces emerged from the roiling brume; women's faces made of fog, soot and smoke, their features caught and frozen in their last moments of Earthly life.

Something else approached, causing the spirit women to spin around in alarm. Annie shrieked in terror as two red eyes like balls of flame glowed through the surrounding miasma. Something inhuman, radiating evil, approached her. Its breath flared with a blue/white flame illuminating a diabolical face of a horned, fiendish man. Clad in tight-fitting, gore-stained leather, the monstrosity had long arms with claw-like hands ending in metallic talons, which dripped with fresh blood. It had no feet but cloven hooves that struck the ground with a powerful thud. With no chance of escape, Annie sobbed, holding onto the gas lamp in the hope that its faint light could save her.

A shudder of movement stirred around her as women made from fog gathered together and stood between the monster and the child. Annie could feel their anger and their strength as a vibration as tangible as her own fear-strangled breath. As the faces and forms gathered more detail, she recognised amongst them the four streetwalkers that used to pass beneath her window.

One spoke, an older woman, a local, her voice audible but distorted as if speaking from a long distance.

'You can't 'ave this little 'un, Jack. Nor any more of us. One or two poor bitches were not strong enuf, but the more yer killed, the more powerful we 'ave got.'

The creature snarled and spat more blue flame that hissed in the damp air, and stepped towards Annie. She could see its thin, gnarled form and diabolical face contorted with predatory hunger. Its hooves stamped the ground in fury, firing sparks off the cobbles.

Again, the fog spirits of the women moved closer to Annie, linking arms and holding their ground. Their spokeswoman challenged the demon, 'You've had yer fill of our blood and guts, Jack. Now it's time fer yer to bugger off aht of Whitechapel. Find some other poor bitches to prey off. Yer all done here.'

The spirit forms began to merge and the air rotated and grew in intensity until it became a whirlwind, punching through the night with preternatural power. Annie clung on to the gas lamp with all her fading strength, while dust and street debris joined the maelstrom buffeting her. The whirlwind became yet more focused, denser; an emotion-charged storm potent with anger, sorrow and regret and sharp-honed with revenge. It slammed against the demon, sending the creature flying through the air in an untidy tangle of limbs. It was swallowed up by the fog, and Annie heard it land some distance away.

The creature struggled back towards her, the fog roiling around its body as it approached, but the women were far from done with it. Screaming their fury, their co-joined whirlwind form blasted into their killer over and over again until it fled into the fog. The sound of its hoof-falls echoed away through the deserted streets.

Traumatised, Annie lay weeping, still clinging to the gas lamp.

A short time later she heard a hue and cry. Another streetwalker had been murdered. With the call came a rush of feet, and Annie fell into the shocked arms of a local constable.

The pandemonium she had created by disappearing into the fog was soon forgotten by her return home, unharmed, wrapped in the constable's coat.

Hours later, the safe arrival of a new baby brother took the family's mind completely away from this momentary terror.

After the birth, Annie's mother sent for her.

'What you did was very foolish but very brave. Lucky yer father came home early 'cos of the choking Particular. So what shall we call 'im? Yer turn to choose,' her mother said as she held up the infant.

Annie kissed the top of the baby's soft, downy head. 'Anything but Jack, Ma. Anything but that.'

Annie's mother looked at her and frowned. She didn't ask the young girl how she knew about the creature the press had dubbed 'Jack the Ripper': some questions were best left unasked. But she feared, like any mother, what her daughter might have seen in the fog. She secretly fretted over some imagined loss of innocence that she had hoped to protect her from.

Exhausted, Annie sought out her bedroom, but the old draw of the gas lamp still lingered. Nervous, her hands shaking as she peeled back the curtain, Annie peered out of the window.

At first there was nothing but the usual swirl of filthy air around the lamp's brave but ineffective umbra. Then one by one, four streetwalkers appeared from the fog. Stepping into the gaslight, for a few seconds their forms regained the cheery, tawdry appearance so familiar to Annie. The women looked up, smiled and waved to her. Then they dissolved slowly into the surrounded fog, and she never saw them again.

IN *INSOMNIUM VERITAS*

London, 1875

A cobweb touch across his hand, a brush of sepulchre breath on his cheek. That was all she gave him. He wanted more … so much more …

Gervaise Foxe lay sprawled, fully dressed, on his floor. His clothes were dishevelled, stinking of London gutters and sweet opium. Like a drowning man grabbing at anything to save his life, Foxe held tightly to the fast-fading memory of his dream encounter. Terrifying yet intoxicating … whoever, whatever she was, his night visitor had made a claim on his soul. One he was so willing to relinquish to be with her.

A timid parlour maid tapped on the door, rousing him from his stupor. Her interruption chased away the torn fragments of his fading memories. Raging at their loss, he bellowed a foul, violent oath at the unwitting, innocent girl.

He grunted, satisfied by her sobs and hurried footsteps as she skittered back down the corridor, and fell back to the floor. *Good. Let there be no more interruptions.*

Heavy drapes of burgundy velvet prevented the brash invasion of daylight. Foxe clambered onto a brocade settle and fell into a light, restless slumber, desperate for another glimpse of the mystery, another revelation of her. Nothing came but a disappointing jumble of mundane images. Shaking them from his mind on awaking, Foxe knew he had to wait until the cover of night fell again on the grandeur of his Mayfair home. Only then could he leave, seek out the same opium den and continue his journey of dissolution and discovery, willingly exchanging more of his soul for greater knowledge of her. Illogical, yes, but Foxe had decided that particular house of vice alone was the portal to her world. One he wanted to remain in.

The leaden, dragging hours of daylight acquired a malign intent, each slow minute pausing, delaying its departure as if wanting to torture and mock Foxe's impatience. So much so, he could not endure for a minute longer the incessant rhythmic beat of the mahogany clock, its long case standing proudly in the corner of the room. Dragging the heavy, offending object across the Persian rug, he heaved it outside onto the corridor floor, where it smashed in a protesting clamour of broken cogs and glass. Satisfied he had defeated one more enemy to his seclusion, he slammed the door to shut out any more disturbances from his household.

Unable to face food or any liquid beyond some bitter wine dregs left in a glass, he tried to occupy his mind: reading, catching up with his correspondence, only to dash the books and papers to the floor in agitation. It was impossible to concentrate. He wanted her, only her.

As night fell, Foxe left the prison of his home. Snow had fallen during his stupor, giving the streets a glamour they did not deserve. Part of his fevered mind recalled it was the eve of the Christmas festivities. This meant nothing to him and never had. The banal orgy of overindulgence and sickening good cheer would not be missed.

He did not call for his own smart carriage – he wanted no witness to his destination – and strode out to seek the hire of a Hansom cab. His excitement rose, exquisite with the pain of longing as the cab swayed and clattered through London's night streets, moving from moneyed elegance to the seething slums of Whitechapel.

As the snow returned in flurries driven by an icy, peevish wind, he arrived outside a rundown Georgian town house, its fading gentility hemmed in by surrounding, overcrowded tenements and encroaching reeking squalor. Evidence of its shame was protected by a swirling fog gloom and no gaslights were set to illuminate its façade.

The driver discreetly reined in the horse as close to the doorway as possible, avoiding exposing his toff passenger to harassment from the street doxies, thieves and beggars out hunting for prey. Fine gentlemen were a common sight on these dank, narrow streets, visiting their molls or the many houses of vice. There was always somewhere and someone to cater for every lurid, secret need.

Foxe rapped on the door with the handle of his cane and a tall, broad shouldered Oriental man allowed him to enter, ushering him through to the inner chambers, polite but radiating his silent contempt for the rich, weak Westerners who sought the den's false promises of paradise. The poisoned air was thick and pungent with the opiate smoke that permeated curtains and clothing with equal persistence. A hush merged with the smoke, and it stank of oblivion and lethargy, along with the sickening breath of the many dreamers.

Foxe barely noticed. He was beyond caring ... this was no more than a threshold, one he must cross to be with her again. The den's owner, an elderly woman addressed by all as Madam Lin, took him to a private chamber, her nose wrinkling in disgust at his rank smell of dried sweat and urine, her flint-sharp eyes narrowing as she took in his rumpled clothes, the same he had worn on his visit the night before. Foxe was aware that these were warning signs to her that he was chasing the dragon with far too much enthusiasm. A fatal overdose and he may end up floating face down in the Thames. She did not want another scandal and there had been so many handsome, wealthy young men lost recently in mysterious circumstances.

He purchased the opiate, pressing his money into Lin's hands, and stuffed it in the pocket of his coat.

Once left alone, Foxe settled, lying on a stained, damp couch and clutching an opium pipe in his hand. He charged the pipe and drew in a deep lungful of opium smoke, feeling it suffuse his lungs and body before he sank into a deep stupor. He managed one more draw from the ornate, green glass and gilded pipe before the tarnished reality of his life gave way to hers ...

A forest path. Narrow. Strewn with ankle-breaking exposed roots and fallen branches. He stood puzzled and angry. What manner of trick was this? From what he could remember of his last visit, he should have been already in her chambers, waiting for her arrival. Was she punishing him with banishment? Foxe stumbled down the track. How could this be a dream? He smelt the astringent tang of pine sap, the rich earthiness of mulch beneath his feet. His feet felt the roots and stones beneath them. And he saw the glimmer of candle-light through the trees. Hope rose: that must be her dwelling. Even she could not be so cruel as to deny him now.

Confidence growing, he strode through the protective stand of dark, mature pines to find an impressive tall building of crumbling stone, traces of its original rich red amid the time-softened soft pink hues. The house was in appearance decrepit yet gracious, impossible to date. This edifice had grown as past owners had added to its structure over the ages. Nature had also changed it, a dense trail of dark ivy creeping across the stones. Curious twisted turrets competed for the eye, as did the jewelled gleam of stained glass, boldly coloured in contrast to the age-worn fabric of their surroundings

A fine house indeed, but there was a melancholy atmosphere of old tragedy and deep, dark secrets seeping from the stones. A taint of danger too. Foxe was beyond caring. If this was her home, then he could face anything to be with her. Inside, somehow he knew there would be many narrow, gloomy corridors leading to mysterious, locked chambers. He had never been here before but it felt like home in a way his grand house in Mayfair never could . He belonged here, in her world.

At first his heart lurched with disappointment, as she had not run out to greet him. Maybe the house was empty? But it felt expectant. He imagined some metaphorical holding of breath as it waited for him to enter and bring it back to life. He paused before the door, gaze drawn to a high window, deep in the recess of a curving buttress. A wraith-like shadow moved, too fleet for him to make out its full form. It filled him with dread. He was certain it could not be his enchantress but something else, something baleful, predatory. Overcome by a sudden urge to leave lest he saw the shadow's face, he turned on his heel and ran back through the forest to the sunlight-dappled river.

Once at its gently sloping banks, he bent down to scoop up some water as if to cleanse himself of the weakening fear. To his astonishment the river rose to engulf him ...

... and he spluttered awake as an insistent Madam Lin shocked him to consciousness with a jugful of ice-cold water thrown in his face.

Devil take the woman!

'Sir,' the opium den proprietor insisted, ignoring his rage. 'Sir, you have taken too much of your pleasure. I will not allow my young gentlemen to perish in this establishment.'

Enraged at the interruption, Foxe staggered to his feet, clutching at the high back of the couch to keep his balance. In truth, his anger was also aimed at himself, for his rank cowardice. How could his enchantress ever forgive him for turning tail and running like a frightened child at the first sign of perceived danger? He had to go back there, now ... undo the damage before she rejected him, left him with this unbearable and unfulfilled yearning.

On unsteady legs, he lurched out of Madam Lin's, pushing past anyone in his way, oblivious to their curses. In the night gloom, with no gaslight to guide his faltering steps, Foxe fell in the street, bruising his knees on the greasy cobbles. He retained enough fading self-awareness to know that he looked like a filthy beggar.

His fine clothes were streaked with street filth and his own dissolution. Madam Lin's was not the only house of vice in the area, but any opium den that enjoyed the patronage of gentlemen would never allow him past its doors.

As the opium smoke lingering from the den now mingled with an oily fog in his lungs he knew where must go. There were many slop houses near London Bridge – always a ready source of laudanum at any hour of the night – and in one of those he could go back to find her, to convince her, he was all hers ... life and soul.

Foxe's hand strayed to his coat pocket, and he realised that the opiate was still there. He hurriedly pulled it out and looked at it. There was no need to seek the comfort and protection of a den or bawd house or risk another interruption: he was on a journey from which he would not return.

Foxe sat down on the frozen, filthy slush in an alley, wedged between some old empty meat boxes left from the day's market, sending two brace of fat, brown rats scurrying. Without hesitation, he pulled a basic pipe from his pockets, charged it, and, with a shaking hand, struck a match, holding it to the opiate until it caught. With a sigh, Foxe drew the smoke into his lungs, and found his last oblivion.

Foxe stood at the door to the mansion. She had rewarded his swift return. Elated, he stepped forward and the door creaked open, releasing tendrils of sorrow and insanity to curl around his legs. He realised this was the last time in life or death Jonas Foxe would have a choice. He could turn and run, immerse himself in the ice water stream and return to his London of 1875. Become once more the respectable gentleman of his standing in society. One day, no doubt, a husband to some simpering, frigid woman of his family's choice and father to wretched, unhappy children he would hardly see as they progressed from nursery to boarding school. End up an Earl, a politician like his father, fighting to keep the ruling establishment at the top of the ladder. The thought of this future scared him far more than the dark and eerie mansion hallway.

He stepped inside.

Foxe knew he was not alone. Indistinct shades lingered at the periphery of his vision, hate-filled, jealous but too insubstantial to harm him ... unless he let their entropy and sorrowing damnation taint his own soul. His contempt of them did not go unnoticed. Bolder ones edged forward, hissing in loathing.

Then, at last, she approached along the hallway behind him. She made no sound but her presence was strong, powerful enough to send the fearful shades scattering away into the deeper shadowed recesses of the house.

She made no footfall, just the rustle and drag of old, torn silk and shredded lace. Foxe forced his eyes shut. He needed her to touch him but he did not want to see what she had become ... not yet. He knew she now stood in front of him; he could smell the decay and dust on her garments. Hear their tomb-born frayed rustle. She leant forward and kissed his lips, at first a meeting of cold bone and dried leather against warm living flesh. Foxe did not baulk. He knew this would change, and it did. Her caress became an enchantment of soft, perfumed skin against his. When he took her in his arms, she was yielding, pliant, adorable. Foxe's hand brushed lightly against her breasts, so full and firm trapped in their tight silken corsetry.

He opened his eyes and at last was able to take in her loveliness. Her grey-green, alluring eyes with their flirtatious long lashes. Her petite figure clad in the extravagant pastel silks and ribbons of an earlier century. Her silver-blonde hair framing her elfin face in long, gleaming ringlets. She gave a coquettish giggle and, taking Foxe's hand, led him deeper through her home, through shade-haunted corridors without gaslight or candles, to her bedroom. He paused, uneasy, not expecting this. She was a lady, an enchantress not some common bawd.

'My beloved, we have so little time. If you want me, it must be now,' she said, her voice soft and low yet almost childlike in its gentle timbre.

Foxe could see her eyes glisten with tears that diamond-sparkled despite the twilight gloom. He did not hesitate … he needed to be deep within her, possessing her body as she stole his life and soul.

Foxe sat beside her on the window seat, brushing away an offending fly creeping across her motionless face, her features now mere bone framed with yellow, dried tatters of flesh. He reached across and took her skeletal hand in his. There he would sit until his body became as dead and desiccated as hers, his predatory spirit wandering through the opium dreams of others with no sensation beyond the sighing breath of the sepulchre and a cobweb touch.

WORSE THINGS HAPPEN AT SEA

London, 1860

The Thames-side mud clung to the scrawny boy's legs in a cold grasp; a clammy, fetid caress laden with threat from hidden danger and disease. The boy was cautious but unconcerned. Young Tom Jenkins was a mudlark, a name perhaps coined by some toff as a term of derision but something the eight year old was proud of.

He and his grandpa Bert answered to no-one. They could scrape a meagre living searching the mud flats of the Thames at low tide for anything they could dig up or scavenge, but everything they owned was theirs. Despite the abandoned nature of their finds, they lived in constant vigilance from the police, who deemed them thieves. The two mudlarks had made a rough dwelling by the side of London's great river, a makeshift, ramshackle construction of broken timber from packing cases fallen into the water. It was a home that could be replaced if washed away by an extra-high tide. Or broken up by the police – that had happened many times, to Bert's impotent rage and Tom's despair. More than once they had spent a cold night sleeping rough. But Bert always rebuilt their shelter through need and defiance.

The lad waded through the mud, which was, as ever, doing its best to suck him down and submerge him beneath its reeking depths. For all his pride, it was filthy work, Tom could not deny that. The Thames was a river of death, awash with rotting debris, dead rats and cats and often dead people and always rank with thick layers of human sewage. Nothing could live in the putrid water that claimed lives every day. Sometimes mudlarks were carried away by the tide, or by illness from the filthy water. Artery-deep gashes were another daily hazard, from broken glass unseen within the glutinous mud. A bad cut became infected every time and took many of Tom's fellows off hopefully to a better world. Tom tried not to let his wild thoughts take over his mind, for sometimes he imagined bony hands grabbing at his ankles, wanting him to share their forgotten grave of shifting mud. Nonsense, of course. As his grandpa said, the dead are dead and do not come back.

But what the rest of London threw away could be scavenged and would buy a hot meal for the mudlarks. It made the risks worthwhile. Coins, artefacts from the river's thousands of years of history, were treasures all who worked the banks sought; and his grandpa, as a lifelong mudlark, was one of the best for finding good stuff.

As ever, Tom also pushed aside sad thoughts of the worse times, such as the Great Stink – when even Parliament across the river had to close down from the stench of ordure from the Thames – and the epidemics of cholera and typhoid that were no respecters of class or wealth. Many in the mudlark community were carried away by disease but so had been the Queen's husband, the German prince. Tom was six at the time of the Stink and the worst epidemics and remembered having to wear a cloth across his nose and mouth to get on with his work. Children he thought of as friends did not always return. He learnt not to get friendly with anyone. He had his grandpa, grumpy, as tough as old leather, seemingly as old as the Thames itself, but who loved him fiercely … Who else would he want in his life?

All this death and danger Tom took in his stride. He knew no other life, never knew his parents. There had always just been Bert and himself and the Thames. The river was a cruel mistress, yielding up treasure one day and taking lives the next. One of the toff scientists from the new museum who paid well for any really old stuff they found – a kindly old man with a foreign accent – told Tom that the river had been named after a Celtic goddess, Tamar. That seemed to make sense to the boy; the river was powerful and capricious enough to be associated with a goddess.

At least they were not toshers; the desperate people who scavenged the sewers for anything of value and who stole copper from the hulls of moored ships. Mudlarks were low on the ladder of society but there were people beneath them. This seemed to give some pleasure to his grandpa. In fact any misfortune that did not happen to him and the nipper was a source of satisfaction to Bert. He would pause, shake his head with a proper show of sadness, then mutter, 'Worse things 'appen at sea, my lad.' What these worse things were Bert never explained, and it was a constant source of puzzlement and wonder to Tom.

Tom glanced up from the cold mud as dawn finally lit up the London skyline. The weak early sun struggled through the constant fug of smoke from the ever-growing sprawling city. He was alone that morning; Bert had taken some good finds to the museum, hoping to raise more money for his retirement.

'It will only take one good 'un,' he would say every time he headed for Kensington, burlap sack over his shoulder. 'One good 'un and we can leave the river forever.'

There had been no other mudlarks around when Tom had first arrived, long before dawn, to claim his pitch even though it was too dark to work. With police raids an ever-present threat, grabbing what they could before the bastards came on duty was essential. This morning Tom had been aware of a ragged young lad standing in the mud further downstream. Tom had called out a cheery greeting but the boy either could not hear him or was too shy to respond. A newcomer perhaps, one driven by desperation to risk his life and health scavenging the river bank. There were certainly signs of hardship and starvation about his stance and gaunt frame, draped in filthy, torn garb that gave no protection from the chill wind that rolled in from the river. Tom was glad of his own brown fustian coat and vest, his tough canvas trousers and roughly-patched striped shirt, topped with an old tweed cap with a peak that kept the rain off.

As other mudlarks arrived, all familiar faces, Tom pushed aside his curiosity over the newcomer and concentrated on dredging through the viscous mud with a rake and his hands, knowing there was never enough time before the river rose and engulfed the bank on which they stood. The children too young to work the banks stood on lookout for the police while the rest of them sought lumps of iron, copper nails, pieces of coal, sail canvas … anything that could be sold for re-use for a few pennies.

Well taught by his grandfather, Tom grabbed what he could from the surface, stuffing it into one of the sacks he wore strapped to his back, then dug deeper to see what the ever-shifting Thames mud concealed, seeking the gleam of silver and gold that could be old coins or jewellery. The everyday stuff kept him and Bert alive; the treasures could mean freedom and a new life.

During his search, Tom occasionally looked up at the new lad, who curiously still stood at the same spot, gazing into the mud but not searching. The others ignored him and so did Tom. The lad would have to quickly learn to get dirty and grub through the washed up debris if he was going to earn a crust or a mug of ale.

They had been searching for some time when one of the little ones blew a shrill whistle to indicate trouble was on the way. Everyone fled with well-practised speed, disappearing into the riverside warren of slums and warehouses like cockroaches startled by light.

The following morning, the strange boy was there again, early and in the same position. Again, he paid no attention to his surroundings but stared into the mud with the same intense concentration. He must have been fast on his feet though, Tom concluded, not to have been caught by the police the day before. Bert's cough of disapproval made his grandson forget the newcomer and concentrate on the task at hand; much time had been lost the day before from the raid. The Thames-side rumours that morning spoke of mudlarks nicking coal from a moored barge, triggering the latest raid. Bert had never done that, but he blamed the barge owners for not protecting their cargo … *fair game*, he called it.

That day they were left undisturbed until high tide

and, though pickings were poor, Bert and Tom had found enough muddy treasure to buy a couple of loaves of bread and a generous slice of cheese. It would be good to go to bed without the painful griping of an empty stomach.

The next morning arrived with a bitter northerly wind. Bert felt unwell and decided to sleep on for another hour, leaving the boy to make a start on the river bank. The icy wind seemed to have reached deep into the mud. Tom shivered at its cold touch around his legs. Now his curiosity was too much to deny as he saw the gaunt form already in place, still with his back turned and gazing down into the mud by the side of the river. Tom called out again in friendly greeting but was again ignored.

This lack of response was deemed downright rude by the mudlark community. They were in competition with each other for finds yet still managed to be a cheery company. Tom had had enough. Leaving his bags on the mud as proof of his occupation of that area, he waded closer to the still figure, ready to challenge him. If the lad was aware of his approach, he gave no sign, though he raised one skeletally thin arm and pointed into the mud, covered by a couple of feet of the lapping river water. Tom looked into the water to see the alluring glint of gold peering through the grey mud; something large, ornate and precious. This could be the one: the treasure Bert had dreamed about all his life.

Tom waded in, muttering, 'If you ain't got the stones to 'ave it for yerself, tough. First law of mudlarks means its mine.'

The boy did not answer as the more experienced mudlark waded into the river. The gleaming object had first appeared close, near the surface, but Tom found he could not reach it as easily as he thought and took another step. The mud was deeper, with a heavier, cloying feel, but it was nothing he hadn't coped with before for something worthwhile, and what could be more worthwhile than this?

He bent over, stretched out with his rake and tried to pull out the object but again it was too far away. It had to be an effect of the rising sun on the water, making it appear closer than it was. That had caught out many a mudlark. Now he could make out the sparkle of gemstones, rubies and sapphires set into the gold. A necklace fit for a queen! Refusing to be denied such life-changing treasure, he waded closer, or at least attempted to. The mud had taken a strong hold on him now, no longer a sticky caress but a determined, malign grip that he couldn't release by moving or prising himself free by leaning on the rake. Stuck fast, his struggles only made the mud hold him tighter, and now his weight was pulling him down, deeper into the treacherous quagmire.

Already sunk down to his knees, Tom yelled out to the silent lad, the only person on the riverbank. Second law of mudlarks was always to help your own kind in danger. When the boy did not respond, Tom twisted around to confront him.

The boy was still there, at least what was left of him.

Reeking of putrefaction, grey-green, ragged flesh hung on bare, stained bones. His face was all but gone, skull emerging through the last scraps of bloated flesh. There were no eyes left but his mouth spread into a broad rictus grin.

Horrified, Tom turned away from the frightful apparition. The tempting necklace was gone and only the reflection of the spectre stared back at him through the brown flow of filthy water. Using the last reserves of his strength and courage, Tom twisted again and swung the rake around to anchor into the firmer mud closer to the bank. The rake passed through the ghastly form, dispersing it like smoke. It hit the firmer mud, and held fast in a tenuous grip that would not last. Weeping, Tom knew it was his only chance. He pulled hard along the rake but his wet, mud-caked fingers could not hold it tight enough and the wooden handle slipped from his grasp.

He fell back, his head dipping beneath the freezing brown water. Unable to get back upright, he felt the Thames flowing high and fast above his head, forcing its way into his nose, his mouth. Unable to fight the river, Tom knew he was drowning. Perhaps he would be washed away with the tide like so many before.

It crossed his mind that he might finally discover what the worse things were that happened at sea …

Deep water lapped over the head of his precious lad but Bert would not let go. The Thames had claimed enough young mudlarks' lives already; she wasn't having this one. He felt others join him, big lads thankfully, mudlarks caring for one of their own. Stronger arms than his pulled Tom clear of the deadly sludge, their rough handling enough to get him coughing and breathing again.

Then he saw him. The ghost boy, a whispered about and feared mudlark legend of many years standing. For a few, ghastly moments the spectral child stood in the deep mud, more bone than flesh. A splintered, putrescent arm reached out to point in the water.

Bert saw the gleam of gold and sparkle of gemstones in the river, berating himself that he had never frightened Tom with midnight tales of Ragged Robin and the blighted lost treasure. He should have warned the boy, kept him safe. Bert looked up from the shining lure, knowing it for false and swore at the malevolence before him. The ghost's part skeletal, part bloated face broke into a terrifying grin before the figure walked deeper into the Thames and disappeared beneath the waves.

Bert gave thanks to a god he did not believe in and began to pull himself out of the tight, clinging mud to get back to the temporary safety of the bank.

But - the river and its spectres were not finished.

An unstoppable impulse made him turn and look back. The ghost boy had returned and was no longer alone. Two adults flanked him. One was the wretched corpse of a young woman, ugly bruises around her neck made more livid by her unearthly pallor. The other was a man, slightly older, the cause of his death obvious by the unnatural angle of his neck and the remnants of a noose around it. Bert recognised them. They were his own murdered daughter and the evil bastard of a son-in-law who killed her and paid the ultimate price. But not by any court of law: the mudlarks administered their own justice.

The revenants reached out their hands, more yellowed bone than water-rotted flesh, and their mouths opened in a wide howl made more dreadful by their silence. Bert knew what they wanted.

'The boy is with me. You cannot have him.'

The spectres of the lad's parents moved toward the bank. Neither the mud nor the water impeded their progress, but some instinct told him they could not leave the river that held their bones; the land was safe. Again they opened their torn and rotting mouths to call out for their son.

'I did you wrong, Rosie. I never told the lad about you or what happened to you,' Bert addressed the female spirit, his heart breaking at what had happened to his girl and his part in hiding her death. 'That at least I can put right. But young Tom does not belong to the river. Not now, not ever.'

Bert turned away, this time he did not look back. He wrapped the shivering child in his coat and, picking up his grandson, turned his back on the dead and waded back to the living.

THE ATTIC NURSERY

London, 1899

Medicine time. Sophia carefully lined her children up, with the youngest first to take their daily dollop of cod liver oil and malt. It was easier that way. If any of the little ones got upset, the elder siblings could comfort them while she carried on dishing out the linctus. She never forgot this daily ritual. It was really important to keep the little ones healthy; there was a nasty illness about. Many people, including some of her friends, were no longer around after getting the sickness. They said nobody was safe, even Kings and Queens could get it. They said that nothing could be done to stop it, that only good luck and prayers kept you out of harm's way. But Sophia was determined to prove them all wrong. She could keep her family safe, keep them well. The sickness had no place here.

She carefully went down the line, mindful of the silky hair ribbons, the pretty ruffles and lacy frills of their clothes, and raised a silver spoon to each little mouth, rewarding their excellent behaviour with a smile and warm hug. They were such good children. Other people's babies were always naughty, getting their clothes filthy and breaking things, but not hers. After the short-lived ordeal of the nightly medicine session, Sophia gave them all a well-earned reward; each was allowed a small, round Parma violet sweet to take away the nasty taste.

Then came the best part of her day. Sophia pulled up a pine rocking chair and bade them all sit down in front of her. Once they were all settled quietly, she read to them, choosing their favourite bedtime story. It was her favourite too, about a beautiful fairy with delicate silver wings that flew all the way to the moon and made friends with a family of jolly pixies. They all loved that story, especially the bit when the plucky fairy rescued a tiny moon baby from falling down a deep crater.

With the story over, Sophia began the cosy ritual of bedtime, washing their faces and hands, brushing out their long silky hair and taking off their daytime clothes to put on their snugly night things. Singing a lullaby, she tucked them up under their thick, brightly-coloured patchwork quilts, each getting a special hug, gently murmured endearments, a kiss – just for them.

Outside, the weather had worsened. Ice-laden rain began to beat against the window driven by a harsh wind that moaned like a poor lost soul forced to wander the Earth searching for a home it would never find. Sophia was not bothered. She was warm and safe, her little ones snug beneath the kaleidoscope patches of their quilts. She sat back down on the rocker, now pulled up beside the row of little beds, and watched them sleep with a smile of sheer contentment. Backwards and forwards went her chair. Tiredness made her eyelids heavy, and lulled by the rhythm of the chair she began to fall asleep.

What was that? A sound downstairs, the sharp click of metal against metal. Sophia's heart jumped in alarm. Loud voices and the scrape of heavy footsteps downstairs against the wooden parquet floor. At first she was frozen with indecision, praying they would go away; perhaps they had made a mistake and entered the wrong house. Maybe they would just leave. But the main door closed with a resolute bang and the footsteps made steady and relentless progress through the house.

Sophia swiftly gathered up her little ones and sought out a place of refuge. Where could she go? What did they want with her? She felt another surge of disabling panic rise through her body, but she could not give in to it. Must not give into it! For the sake of her family, she knew she must stay calm, be so very brave. Like the fairy with the silver wings.

To her relief, the footsteps grew fainter at first, as the intruders headed to the kitchen down in the basement, where they seemed to dwell the longest. This gave her the gift of precious time, enough time to hide. At least she had the older ones with her – they could help keep the babies quiet.

She found the ideal spot, a deep, empty cupboard built into the back of the nursery, and hurried everyone inside, closing the door tight shut despite her trembling hands. Fear made her body quiver uncontrollably but she forced herself to stay calm for the sake of the children, drawing her knees right up to her chin, the youngest two in her arms, held so tightly. Putting her fingers to her lips, urging the others to stay quiet, as quiet at the smallest house mouse being stalked by a ferocious kitchen cat.

Despite Sophia's hastily whispered prayers, the intruders were not going away. Their voices got closer and louder; close enough now to make out it was two deep masculine voices and one much lighter – a woman. They had left the kitchen and were going slowly from room to room, pausing in each to talk, though it was still too far away for Sophia to make out what they were saying, to find out what they were doing breaking into her house.

They eventually reached the floor below but were closing in. Again, at a leisurely pace, they walked from room to room. Sophia found it hard to breathe, though she knew the cupboard was spacious and empty. Fear tightened her chest and closed up her throat. The darkness crowded in on her like a crushing leaden pall. Then in horror she remembered that little Esme, the baby, sometimes cried out when she lost her balance. Sophia grabbed her, held the infant close to her body, pleading silently for the little one to stay quiet, to fall asleep.

With sickening inevitability, the invaders finally climbed the short flight of narrow stairs and walked boldly into the nursery. With the darkness closing in, tighter and tighter, Sophia gathered up all her children in an even firmer hold and bit down hard on her knuckles, drawing blood in an unseen trickle through her fingers. Anything to stop the high whimper of terror struggling to escape from her throat and betray them all.

'Brrrr – this is a cold place,' muttered the woman.

'Nothing bringing central heating up here wouldn't fix,' countered her companion cheerily. 'I think this could make a useful extra bedroom, or a study. Imagine it with pine flooring, a dormer window and roof lights.'

The woman walked around, her heels making a staccato rhythm on the bare floorboards. 'It's such a sad little room, stuck right at the top of the old house, somewhere forgotten and forlorn. I don't like it.'

She turned and strode out briskly, her partner, puzzled and apologetic, following quickly in her wake.

'Yet another sale down the toilet,' muttered the other man with a resigned sigh. He paused to glance around the attic nursery with a baleful glare before his nerve gave out and, with a shudder, he hurried down the stairs to follow his clients out of the large Victorian pile that no-one from his firm of estate agents could shift.

Alone again.

It was time to give the little ones their medicine. Sophia lined up her dolls and raised the silver spoon to each painted mouth. Outside the ice rain lashing the attic window had turned hard and sleety like scratching fingernails. The cold weather was a good sign. It meant Christmas would be here soon. Maybe she would get another baby to join her family.

She sat the dolls down in a line and began to read their favourite story. Her favourite too. The one about the fairy and the pixies who lived on the moon.

THE GREEN GOWN

Paris, 1891

Pierre Antoine Lauzier kept his head down as he alighted from his train at Paris Gard Du Nord. Bracing himself to tackle the crowds, mind already resigned to the day's employment stooped over tedious records in the government office of taxation, he braved the wind-driven sleet beyond the shelter of the rail station and walked along the platform.

He had no idea why he looked up, a quirk of fate perhaps? Lauzier saw a fleeting flash of bright green through a swirl of smoke and steam from a departing locomotive. It was a young woman walking alone towards the exit with a proud yet hesitant bearing. Her dark hair and pale face were barely hidden by a delicate green lace veil. Dragged down by the tedium of his life, Lauzier could not bear to let this vision of beauty, youth and fresh spring disappear into the milling throng. In a fit of uncharacteristic spontaneity, he ran along the platform, eager to see her again. Somehow her appearance lifted his soul; he needed another dose of this strange medicine before submerging himself into the daily drudgery of his employment.

Of course he would not approach her; even a lowly taxation clerk could be a gentleman. There was nothing about her appearance that spoke of anything but a well-bred young lady, despite the curious lack of a chaperone. Her walk had none of the proud confidence of a gypsy or the predatory hip sway of a streetwalker. He caught sight of her again on the bustling station concourse. She was no country girl either. Her emerald gown was either an expensive Worth original or a well-crafted copy, garb only a wealthy Parisienne could afford. Even more reason to keep his distance. She was from far too elevated a class for Lauzier to approach. He found himself wishing she would drop a kerchief or perhaps a purse so he could retrieve it; a simple act of basic chivalry was something that transcended the barriers of class and etiquette. An uncomplicated fleeting moment of contact that would send his soul soaring.

Lauzier lost all sense of reason and time. He should have made his way to his office; his superiors brooked no bad timekeeping or excuses. Instead he stayed, using the successive waves of commuting crowds to hide his presence. At first, the young woman looked excited, expectant, her cornflower blue eyes gazing around her as she stood by a coffee stall. Who was she waiting for? Why were they taking so long? As Lauzier's vigil became more concerned, her eager expectancy grew to unease. Whoever she waited for was late. Her distress triggered within Lauzier's heart a protective need to comfort her, but there was little he could do without causing her more alarm. He waited another half-hour, fuming at society's strictures, while this young woman became increasingly tearful and agitated.

Another approaching locomotive hid her behind a shroud of soot-laden steam. As it cleared, Lauzier saw that she was gone. Hopefully she was walking away in the safe company of family members or a husband. With no reason to linger, the young man steeled himself for the anger of his superiors and made his way to the tax office.

La Dame Chance gave Lauzier a rare, fortunate gift that morning. He found no gaunt, wizened, disapproving presence standing guard before his desk. Monsieur Lapin, the tyrant usually in charge of his department, was on leave. In his place was temporary stand-in Gaston Le Fevre, an elderly man nearing retirement and, it appeared, a wistful old romantic at heart. On hearing of Lauzier's chivalrous vigil, he clapped the young man on the shoulder, wiping away a sentimental tear with a silk kerchief. 'This is *La Belle Époque* and spring is not far away. Of course a young man should turn his heart to love.'

Lauzier returned to his desk, his low spirits temporarily buoyant, and within hours life returned to its normal, humdrum pattern. Over the next few weeks, the young man often looked for the woman at the station, knowing it was futile. Why would she return and still be in the same gown? As the weeks became months, Lauzier forgot his vision in spring green, and before the year had turned full circle, he received a promotion and a new office with a more amenable supervisor. The higher salary and status enabled him to become engaged to Mlle Celestine Duval, the pretty, timid daughter of a distant cousin.

Ice-spiked rain driven hard by a malign westerly gale had assaulted the windows and roof of Lauzier's carriage throughout the journey into central Paris. Only when the locomotive entered the high-vaulted, ornate shelter of the Gard du Nord did the noisy battering cease. A temporary truce; Lauzier still had to battle the determined spite of the storm as he left the station to walk to his office. There would be no fragile shelter beneath his umbrella; the strength of the wind would wrench it inside out or tear it from his hand. Lauzier alighted from the carriage and glanced up at the central clock. He was on time, and all was well.

A flash of bright green caught his eye, and Lauzier's mind spun with a rush of old memories as he watched the same young woman in her beautiful gown walk through the station along the same track, becoming lost briefly in the blast of smoke and steam. All of his past fascination returned in a tidal wave of unreason. This time he would not lose sight of her. What if this was a sign from fate that she was destined to be his? He must make contact with her!

With all thoughts of the meek little mouse Celestine erased from his mind, Lauzier hurried toward the slender figure. Once again she headed for the place by the coffee stall, and once again she waited with a look of happy expectation. A sudden thought struck Lauzier, and he glanced at the date on the newspaper tucked under his arm, confirming that this was the exact anniversary of the date he had first seen the young woman. So this was most likely a regular rendezvous, a celebration with a loved one or family member of some annual event; a birthday perhaps. Possibly for someone who loved seeing her in that particular green dress, so she wore it again as a favour. Despite his earlier urge to talk to the young woman, he realised once more how inappropriate that would be. She was clearly in no danger, so he left with a wistful smile of regret for what was never meant be. He was an engaged man, after all.

Another year passed and Lauzier was now a married man with the arrival of his first child but four months away, God willing. But he had made a note in his diary of the day he might hope to see the woman in the green gown at the station, a curious obsession for which he had no explanation. And indeed, on that very day, on a bright, sharp winter's morning, Lauzier again caught a familiar glimpse of green as the girl made her way through the usual busy crowd of travellers. Curiosity burned in his soul, strong enough to scorch away the restrictions of good manners, class and marital status. This year he had to talk to her, to discover the reason for her annual assignation in Paris.

He followed her at greater speed, pushing past passengers and traders with a rough indifference totally out of character, ignoring their protests and cursing. His sole focus was the slender form making her way to the coffee stand. Once there, his old hesitancy and deeply-ingrained respectability returned to rein in his rash behaviour. He waited, watching from behind his newspaper, determined to discover who her yearly assignment was with. This time he waited longer than the first, when he had felt within a whisker of losing his employment. That risk had not abated but Lauzier was transfixed. Mesmerised. He was determined to see this annual drama played out to the end.

After a while, the young woman's eager anticipation turned from anxiety to despair and hand-wringing. Tears ran unchecked down pale cheeks from cornflower blue eyes that remained lovely and beguiling beneath the flimsy green veil. Biting the knuckles of her right hand in abject misery, she turned from her vigil and ran down the nearest platform.

Alarmed by this unexpected turn, Lauzier gave chase, a tight knot of dread forming in his heart. Through an approaching grey cloud of surging steam, a locomotive headed for the station, its huge iron wheels thundering down the track. To Lauzier's horror, the woman teetered at the edge of the platform, her balance precarious. Her intention was clear. He ran toward her, silently so as not to alarm her and send her over the edge from the shock of being startled. At this point, a braver man than he would have grabbed her waist and pulled her back from the brink of disaster. But Lauzier hesitated.

As he reached her side, he finally spoke. 'Mademoiselle, I beg you, move away from the edge, I cannot bear to see you in such danger.'

She turned. Her face was no longer pretty but grey and gaunt, skull-like, with the skin stretched so tightly over bone that it seemed as though it would tear at the merest touch. Instead of a pair of lively blue eyes, there were blank, sightless hollows. Her face was creased into an expression of pure fury.

Horrified, Lauzier stepped back, gasping as he realised he could see right through the now ripped and blood-stained green gown, could watch the nearing locomotive through her body as it turned as insubstantial as the smoke and steam around them. With a cry of anguish that tore through his soul, the woman leapt in front of the very real train.

Lauzier choked back a shocked scream. Then, staggering back toward the platform's edge, he stared down at the track as the steam from the passing train began to clear. His throat tightened and his heart pounded, while his mind was a turmoil of emotions with the shock of the girl's horrific transition as well as his narrow escape from certain death beneath the train. Nightmare had become a reality and he looked over the platform's edge expecting to see something tangible, something his fevered mind could comprehend.

There was no cruelly-maimed body, no blood, not even a scrap of green silk. Lauzier's gorge rose, the horror turning his fear-weakened legs to pistons of instinctual flight. Barging through the crowds once more, oblivious to their curses and the bruises sustained from many collisions, Lauzier reached the bright exterior of the Gard du Nord, finding sanctuary in the cold winter sun. He held onto a lamppost, his legs too weak to hold him upright. White-faced, crazy-eyed, he had become the focus of horror and alarm from the crowds, but Lauzier was beyond caring.

A form of comprehension gradually seeped through his panic and terror. Of course there was no torn body beneath the train, reasoned his mind, finally accepting that the lady in green was a tragic phantom, a victim of some past misfortune. As reason recovered its dominance of his mind, he thought her far more than a sad revenant. Something far worse. A braver man would have made a grab for her at the platform edge. A braver man would have grasped only thin air and fallen to his death beneath the locomotive.

Lauzier wiped sweat from his brow. His pounding heart beat blood into his ears, deafening him to the sounds of the street, while the horror of his near-death experience truly dawned on him.

He suddenly knew that he had been her intended victim, but fear had held him back and saved his life.

71

His mind replayed the last three years, recalling how his obsession had grown. With every sighting of her, he had found it harder to resist. Next time, he wondered, he might even fall down onto the track in his misguided desire to save her. He might even forget the poison he saw in her putrefying expression.

As he stumbled away, hailing a Hansom to take him the rest of the way to his office, Lauzier looked back at the station. He could still feel those hollow, empty eyes looking into his soul. He had stared death in the face, and part of him had wanted to go there. He knew then, that next year on this day he would take the earlier train to Paris.

He must never again risk catching sight of the girl in the green gown.

AN INSPECTOR FALLS

Old Scotland Yard, London, 1863

A white-faced young constable brought shocking news. Sergeant Corbel took the note and shook his head; a bad case, by all reckoning. His superior, well at least in title, Inspector Gervaise Garamond, unfolded his considerable height from a chair and gestured for Corbel to read the note.

'A bad 'un sir,' the older man muttered. 'An unfortunate scullery maid found stabbed to death in her employer's kitchen. Still had ten knives in her body.'

Garamond paused for a long time to let the message sink in. He was a stick-thin, gaunt man in his early forties, hawk-like in demeanour though not in alacrity of thought. Eventually he attempted to pace dramatically up and down his office; a doomed plan as it was too small, and there were inevitable casualties as documents, pens and inkpots were swept to the floor by his plaid frock coat – a garment in a peculiar shade of green and orange attesting to a troublesome colour blindness … or poor taste, Corbel was never sure on that one.

'Foul play of a most heinous nature,' the Inspector

pronounced, grandstanding to an audience of one. Three if you counted the spiders on the ceiling.

'Possibly, sir,' Corbel added, suppressing a sly grin.

'Ah indeed, yes … only possibly. Only a fool would take such information at face value. There could be many causes of this poor woman's untimely demise …'

Corbel decided to help him out. 'Like suicide?'

This fired Garamond's imagination. 'Suicide, suicide … the last, tragic act of a desperate and wronged young woman.'

Again he began the futile pacing, this time his elbow dislodging from the fireplace a plaster bust of the Queen, which the fast reflexes of Corbel managed to save after a heroic leap for a man of his age and considerable girth. In truth, he was fed up replacing the seemingly endless succession of doomed monarchs. Corbel once replaced one of the Victorias with a bust of Napoleon Bonaparte. The surly Corsican had gone unnoticed by the Inspector even until it too met a messy demise on the tiled office floor.

'Of course it could indeed be suicide. Or …' the Sergeant could almost see the cogs turning in Garamond's brain, 'maybe a tragic accident.'

This revelation set Garamond's mind spinning. This was always awkward as, since he had given up pipe smoking, he liked to bite down on something as he cogitated, and Corbel had hidden all the fountain pens. He didn't want another messy ink incident. The black staining around the Inspector's mouth and chin taken many weeks to fade and had to be put down to a rare tropical complaint contracted on a difficult case. What Corbel told people was: 'Congolian Squid

Syndrome'. With this past embarrassment in mind, the Sergeant swiftly produced a substitute, an unlit old pipe that he now placed within Garamond's grasp. As ever, it did the trick.

'Sergeant, I can see the scene with great clarity ...' Garamond's dark eyes flared with inspiration. 'The maid is about her duties, sitting at the kitchen table, polishing the household cutlery. A cat leaps up to the table, upsetting the tray of knives, which fly through the air and impale the victim. No foul play at all!'

'A cat?'

Garamond gave his Sergeant a pitying look. How slow this man could be in the face of his quicksilver genius?

'Yes, undeniably. A cat. What sensible kitchen would be without a skilled mouser? And being no doubt spoiled by the staff with food scraps, it would become stout and heavy enough to upend the tray.'

The Inspector strode towards the door. 'Come on, Corbel, we have little time to lose. We can solve this mystery in a matter of hours. Let us make haste to Kensington in pursuit of a fat cat.'

They stepped outside Scotland Yard into the gloom of an exceptionally dense pea souper, the London Particular at its most unpleasant. The lights from the row of gas lamps were little more than a series of small dim orbs that did nothing to illuminate the pall. Much to the vexation of the local moth population forced to flutter around the wan light in small, tight circles, leading to many fatal collisions.

Footsteps and hoof beats were muffled, so that passers-by loomed out of the fog only to disappear again seconds later like spectres. Undeterred by this common occurrence in London, especially with the Yard so close to the Thames, Garamond instructed his sergeant to call him a cab. Corbel responded by muttering 'You are a cab, sir' under his breath. Something he said on a daily basis and was just as unfunny as the first time. But every little victory helped.

After 20 frustrating minutes of missing passing vehicles in the all-pervading gloom, Corbel risked life and limb to walk into the street each time he heard the approaching clatter of iron-shod hooves on cobblestones and all but grab the nearest carriage-horse by the reins to halt it. Having endured the curses of two drays hauling beer barrels and a nobleman's landau, on his fourth attempt Corbel managed to stop a Hansom for hire, and the two men were on their way to Kensington. Again Corbel muttered, loud enough for his boss to hear, 'Thank you, Sergeant. That was bold and fearless of you, risking life and limb to halt this cab.'

Garamond was oblivious, his stiletto-sharp mind lost in contemplation of the mystery of the dead scullery maid, his narrow brow furrowed in deep thought. Ten minutes into the journey, he paused from his deliberations and turned to Corbel.

'By Jove, Sergeant … This is a disaster. I have left my pipe back at the Yard.'

Corbel suppressed a sigh. 'You have given up smoking, sir. About a year ago.'

'Of course,' Garamond replied in a curt tone. 'I knew that. Just testing your powers of observation, old friend. Keeps you on your toes.'

They arrived at their destination with a minimal number of street urchins squashed beneath the Hansom's wheels; though in truth, it was partly their fault for migrating from the sea. Nor had they bowled over any wagtails disorientated by the heavy fog. They had, though, nearly knocked down some prostitutes worse for wear from cheap gin. The call in Parliament for a law insisting all females of the street wore bells in their bustles on foggy nights had failed miserably. Another disastrous attempt at law-making from Dotum's Tory MP, Sir David Martlet-Bold. The politician had not learnt his lesson from the notorious debacle of the Bill he had introduced to make only stout children work as chimney sweeps. His insistence that a large lad could clean the chimney more efficiently than a scrawny one had been doomed – just like the lardy lad sent up to demonstrate the MP's theory.

Outside the gracious townhouse, scene of the scullery maid's frightful fate, a stalwart team of local constables kept the gawkers at a set distance; these were professional ones who had passed all their exams in surly muttering, rumour spreading and crowd agitation. Two had even passed their advanced diploma in pitchfork and blazing torch wielding. There was no need of this last service today, thought Corbel, not when the Inspector inevitably and foolishly pronounced the death a sad, unusual accident.

'Stirling work, constables,' said Garamond as he swept passed the cordon. 'I will have this situation solved within minutes and you can be home with your families ere long.'

The constables doffed the front of their helmets in reply but did not hold their breath. Garamond was the last person they wanted to be sent from the Yard. They, the locals, passers-by and the gawkers settled down for a long period of waiting about and muttering.

Once inside, the police officers were greeted by a line-up of tearful staff led by a condescending and oleaginous butler who was introduced by a constable as one Mr Bookman. He was an old-style patriarch of the household staff, whose word was law. So old-style that he wore the outdated livery of the past century, a moth-eaten, once-white wig askew on his round pate, knee-high silk britches painfully tight on his well-fed form. This had the unfortunate appearance of forcing the butler into walking in a cramped, mincing manner as if he had wet himself. When he requested that the police officers 'walk this way,' Corbel had to bite into his knuckles to stop sniggering, especially as Garamond took the words literally. It was going to be a long morning.

The body lay sprawled in a lake of drying blood on the kitchen floor. Someone had thrown a now gore-soaked blanket over the unfortunate woman but it did nothing to hide the horror of her demise or the many knives impaling her like a butterfly specimen on a collector's board. Garamond began to prowl around the room looking for clues; obscure and unlikely ones, as was his way. The Sergeant noted there was no tray of knives, upset or otherwise, and no sign of a resident cat. It was a case of suicide after all, Corbel decided with a huge dose of inner sarcasm.

As Garamond examined a kitchen shelf, inspecting a cream jug in the shape of a cow that had caught his attention, the Sergeant considered the manner of the maid's savage slaying. One knife wound in her body would suggest a moment of madness or desperation from her killer, a burglar caught in the act of stealing the family silver. Several wounds from one knife and a crime of passion became the more likely candidate. Corbel bent down and gently lifted the blanket from the woman's face. He winced. Not a crime of passion then.

The number of knives used suggested something

more outrageous; the vile work of a raving lunatic. There was something almost ritualistic about their placing in her body. Some fiendish cult? Devil worshippers? This had become more popular when one of the dear Queen's sons had come out to the world as a princely Satanist the previous year. Nothing like a bit of royal endorsement for something to catch on in the general populace. Like the Duchess of Cambria's short-lived penchant for wearing hats adorned with stuffed mice. Not all her trend-hungry followers could afford the services of a taxidermist. Clouds of flies buzzing around their hats was soon deemed a fashion *faux pas*.

Garamond had decided the cow creamer was of no significant importance to the case and was now using an overlarge magnifying glass, examining the cooking range for clues.

Meanwhile, Corbel took to interrogating the staff, one by one and on their own, to the outrage of the butler; skivvies and under-footmen were not meant to have opinions of their own. He learnt nothing to arouse his suspicions. The victim was a hard-working and long-serving member of staff, with no vices, hidden or otherwise, and no shady relatives or friends. Neither did the woman have any enemies. She had been a pleasant, simple woman who got on with life and made the best of her humble position.

The sound of a loud furore cut short Corbel's examinations, and he left the kitchen parlour to discover a large woman crammed into her underpinnings like an over-stuffed sausage. From her expansive pure silk gown, vast elaborate bustle and bonnet crammed with half a rain forest's worth of exotic feathers, Corbel deduced this was the lady of the house. Her round, puffy cheeks were flushed with agitation, with three chins wobbling in co-ordinated indignation.

'I am Lady Constantia, Countess of Trebuchet, and I demand to know why Her Majesty's Constabulary are swarming all over my house. Who is in charge of this outrage?'

Corbel's heart sank as the Inspector put down his magnifying glass and gave a rather low, fawning bow.

'Our most sincere apologies for disrupting the smooth running of the household,' the Inspector grovelled, 'but one of your staff has been found bereft of life on the kitchen floor. We are duty bound to investigate the fate of Miss Euphemia Franklin.'

'But I only saw her this morning. I gave her my husband's extra sharp, pointy, dangerous hunting knives to clean.'

The incongruous sound of loud purring drew Corbel's gaze down to the Countess's feet, where the biggest, fattest ginger tomcat he had ever seen wove and slinked around her skirts.

'Ah Pickwick, my little pusskin, you naughty boy. He's not supposed to come down to the servants' quarters, you know. Always jumping up where he doesn't belong.'

Corbel stifled the urge to scream and punch something, preferably Garamond's smug smirk as he bowed once more in an even more obsequious fashion.

'And the knife tray? Where is that?' Corbel spluttered, unable to dismiss his suspicion of foul play so easily.

Bookman stepped forward. 'On discovering it on the floor, I tidied it away. The Countess cannot abide sloppiness in her home.'

The Inspector grabbed Corbel's arm and manhandled him out of the kitchen, still bowing and scraping.

'Your Highness, we will bother you no more, this tragic case is solved. The poor woman met her end as a result of an unfortunate and unpreventable accident. No cats will be charged.'

A TASTE OF ALMONDS

London, 1868

It started with the rats. Just before Christmas too, huge damn things driven up from the frozen Fleet by intense cold, turning the hidden river into a stone-hard glacier beneath the streets and houses above it. Big as cats and bold as beggars, some of the brown invaders took refuge in the Bleakleys' cellar, venturing up to the pantry and kitchen by night and day, helping themselves to food, behaving as unwelcome, unmannerly houseguests.

She blamed him of course. Everything was Ernest Henley Bleakley's fault. It was his contrary choice to move to Clerkenwell on their marriage and not the more factual constraints of fortune and proximity to his employment. No, according to Sarah, his wife of 12 years, he had chosen the house close to the Fleet purely to vex her. Was there anything he did that did not vex Sarah?

Unable to afford servants, it was Bleakley's duty to rid their house – he never used the term 'home' – of the invading vermin. He hoped the apothecary he passed every morning on his short journey to his employment would be open. And so, after helping himself to a wearisome and rank breakfast of a plate of cold mutton, a scraping of the fatty bits left over from the small joint they had shared four days ago on Sunday, Bleakley left early for work.

Bleakley always enjoyed his daily stroll to Heathby's in Birchin Lane, proudly trading as a print works since 1750 and still owned by the same family. Though a bustling, busy part of London, Clerkenwell retained its village atmosphere. It was possible to get to know the other inhabitants, smile and make pleasant small talk, even with the many new Italian immigrants drawn to the area's many esteemed clock-making workshops. He also enjoyed his job, fascinated by the books and pamphlets the company produced. With only a rudimentary education, Bleakley furthered his knowledge at work. His diligence and enthusiasm was noted by his employers and rewarded. He had prospects.

As he braced himself against the seeming solid wall of frozen air that forced him to breathe through his scarf and pinched his exposed face with spiteful fingers, Bleakley knew he was almost happy living here. He loved his work, but returning home always left him dour and depressed, worsening as he entered the front door as if a decade of pent up emotions could be trapped in the iron key.

McGregor's, Apothecary Requisites Par Excellence was indeed open for business, and Bleakley was welcomed by its solemn, black-clad proprietor, curiously named Dr Brown, for there was no sign of any certificate on the shop's walls attesting to his medical qualifications. Nor was there a reason stated why the business was named McGregor's. Bleakley considered it ill manners to query the man's claim to the title, as he suspected did all his customers. The print worker explained about the shameful infestation of rats to Dr Brown, who spoke with the same understanding tone as an undertaker, indeed in his funereal attire, he also resembled one.

'My dear sir, our proximity to the Fleet Ditch brings such unpleasantness to everyone's door, whether prince or pauper. Nothing a taste of almonds would not cure.'

Noting his customer's raised eyebrow of query, he continued, 'Cyanide, sir, it has the smell of bitter almonds, most distinct. And most effective in ridding you of unwelcome lodgers.'

Bleakley made his purchase and continued on his way to work. A pleasant morning productively turned into dinner time, and though Bleakley was close enough to return home for his repast, he chose to frequent the Red Lion inn, a place of good ale, excellent hot food and the cheery company of the widowed landlady, a Mrs Tansy Summerling. How he loved her name, redolent of hazy, warm days spent lying with her in hay meadows strewn with wild flowers, swallows wheeling in the sky and the lazy droning of honeybees. Pure fantasy of course but one he used to sustain him through the bad times. The many bad times.

Later that night, he finally steeled himself to return to his house, all the good feelings engendered by his day dissolving with every step leading to the dwelling. The night was clear and another hard frost had coated the streets with diamonds, but the welcome, as he stepped through his front door, was far colder.

There was no sign of Sarah, a fact he was grateful for. He suspected she had retreated to her own bedroom rather than face him.

Had it always been so? Bleakley had some fading memories of a pert, young woman with sparkling blue eyes, so slender he could encircle her waist with both hands. When had this changed? Or had his love blinded him to reality? That the sparkling eyes were really glacially cold, glittering with a desperate need to escape her repressed life with harsh, strict and puritan parents? That her smiles were part of the entrapment and her lips had always been as thin, pursed and disapproving as her mother's.

Sarah's desire to escape ended on her wedding night, the straitjacket ties of her upbringing that had bound her were unable to be loosened. She had lain in the marriage bed, bony and rigid as a bundle of kindling, refusing to accept his love-struck, gentle caresses and turning her face away from his kisses. Bleakley left her alone that night but any further attempts at intimacy led to disaster. The final straw came when she saw his aroused manhood for the first time and had fled the bed shrieking in horror, vomiting on the carpet in the corridor outside their bedroom. Bleakley did not bother her again.

She had not left him any supper but Bleakley had prepared for this by enjoying a large dinner at the inn and was content with preparing himself a couple of slices of stale bread thinly spread with preserve. He had intended to wash this down with tea but the weariness of his life sent him to his drawing room and the comfort of a measure of brandy. The first taste told him a new tale; the liquor had been watered down. With no servants, there was only one person who could have adulterated the brandy, his wife.

So, Sarah had finally broken one of her many strict rules and partaken some of the demon drink. Bleakley was unsure why but this revelation gave him considerable pleasure. Unable to enjoy the diluted brandy, he put out the cyanide poison for the rats and went to bed.

His slumber, another treasured escape into dreams, occasionally joyous, erotic ones of Tansy Summerling, was shattered by piercing screams. He dressed hurriedly and ran to the inevitable source of the commotion: the kitchen and pantry. Sarah stood outside in the corridor, whiter faced than usual, her arm outstretched towards the kitchen, contempt and accusation distorting her pinched features.

'I hold you responsible for this foulness and horror, Bleakley!'

He glanced in and saw the stiff and contorted bodies of several rats littering the floor. They had not passed peacefully but slowly, writhing in agony. Bleakley felt a twinge of guilt. The creatures held no malice towards their human hosts and were no more than successful opportunists who had entered the wrong dwelling.

'I did what you asked, solved our problem with the vermin.'

Impossible as it seemed, his wife's voice had grown ever more shrill. Bleakley kept his own voice calm, his tone even and conciliatory, pushing down his rising hatred. What good would that do? He was tied to this woman until death. In fact he had even considered a life of debauchery and sinning so that he could go to Hell and avoid her company in the afterlife. At least Hell would give him a warmer welcome.

'The rats would not have entered the house in the first place if you had been more vigilant or were not so lazy. If you worked harder, you could have a better position and be able to hire servants to deal with this matter.'

The old complaint, the old bitterness. She brought up his shortcomings as a breadwinner at every opportunity. He never answered her accusations, there was no point. There was nothing he could say that would assuage her ire and disappointment. It had become a part of her being, as much as her skin and bone.

'I'll clear up the mess,' he replied with the quietest of sighs.

Later, as he took his midday repast at the pub, he related the incident with the brandy bottle to Tansy as he enjoyed a large portion of shepherd's pie and a pint of good ale. She found the thought of Bleakley's shrew wife sneaking measures of brandy and diluting the rest highly amusing. She gave the beleaguered man a friendly pat on the shoulder and advised him with a knowing wink.

'I'll sell you some of my secret supply of absinthe. That will fox her. Try adding water to the Green Fairy and the colour will change from emerald to a pale, milky green. Let us see how your missus wriggles out of that!'

Absinthe. The powerful spirit was looked down on and feared by those of respectable English society, a symbol of French decadence and louche living, but the tiny ember of rebellion smouldering away in Bleakley's soul flared into a fragile spark. The very presence of a bottle of absinthe would enrage Sarah, but he was master of his own house. He would put his foot down and insist.

Once again, after work, he returned to a chill house and punishment in the form of no waiting supper. Still pleasantly full, he retreated to the drawing room and made up a cheery fire in the hearth. He pulled out the bottle of absinthe from his carpet bag and studied the emerald spirit as he held it up to the dancing light of a candle. There was something wonderfully alluring; the wayward, rebellious spirit of the Green Fairy called out to him, seducing him with promises of decadence and escape. He opened it, releasing strange, exotic scents of wild herbs grown on foreign soils. Pouring a small measure into a glass with a shaking hand, he took a hesitant, nervous sip, instantly recoiling at the strength of the alcohol and the alien taste of aniseed.

Remembering Tansy's instruction to temper the spirit with water, he tipped a little into the glass and watched, intrigued as the gradual magical transformation occurred from emerald green to an opalescent white. He took a couple of tentative sips but was disappointed. Bleakley decided he did not like the taste of absinthe, and with fatigue and the slumber-inducing heat from the roaring fire, he slipped into a deep sleep.

Even the small amount of absinthe was enough to awaken the Green Fairy within Bleakley's mind and soul. She tantalised him with dreams of endless possibilities, the visions intoxicated him, made him giddy with joy, as carefree as a young child. He revelled in happiness free of the dour chains that kept him imprisoned in misery. Dancing naked on a warm summer's night beneath a full moon in Tansy's welcoming arms felt so real, so right …

He awoke in the early hours of the morning, cold and stiff in his armchair, the fire long turned to cold ashes. Reality came as a crushing blow. Stumbling up to his bedroom to grab a couple of hours' sleep in the comfort of his bed, he did not notice the now empty glass beside his armchair.

Throughout the day back at work, his mind replayed tantalising memories of the night's dreams, torturing him with their promise of freedom and happiness. Changes churned within him. Bleakley knew he could not allow his life to continue as before. Something had to be done. Over his lunchtime beer, the ideas twisted and changed. Should he just run away and start life again in some new location, even a new country? Should he declare his desire for Tansy Summerling and ride out the resulting scandal? But unknown to Bleakley, the tempting *La Fee Verte* had given him dreams but not common sense. Or the courage to act on them.

On his return to his parlour sanctuary, a bottle of new, unopened brandy under his arm, Bleakley moved the now unwanted absinthe to one side. He paused. Surely there had been more of the green liquid before; he had taken only a small sample. He examined the bottle carefully, breaking into a grin; His terrible spouse had taken a liking to the spirit. Could this be the sign he needed?

He remembered the current craze for emerald green in all things decorative, fabric for clothing, wallpaper … all brought about by the addition of Scheele's Green, a dye derived from arsenic. Bleakley remembered printing a pamphlet the year before from a doctor decrying its use and blaming it for much illness and deaths in the populace. The colour was similar to undiluted absinthe; similar enough to go undetected? If Bleakley did away with his unwanted burden, any police scientist suspecting poisoning would discover copious supplies of cyanide in the house but none in his wife's body. Unlike cyanide, as yet no test had been invented to discover the presence of arsenic. And he worked at a printer's that kept a ready supply of the colourful dye. This was fate showing him the way to future happiness, it had to be.

Over the next few days, a light-hearted and confident Bleakley set about putting his heinous scheme into action. He bought yet more cyanide from the local apothecary, moaning vociferously about the continued problem with ditch rats from the Fleet. He also secreted small amounts of Scheele's Green from his employment in glass vials hidden in his coat pockets. Once at home, Bleakley's heart missed a beat as he first poured the contents of a vial into the absinthe. Any sign of paling and the plan would fail; but the spirit retained its lustrous emerald glow. Perfect.

He carried on his life as before, doing nothing that would raise any suspicion, even to the extent of dining at another inn to avoid been seen in the merry company of his beloved Tansy Summerling. After a week, with no sign of his wife showing any obvious ill health despite evidence she was helping herself to the absinthe, he upped the dosage of Scheele's Green. Bleakley was frustrated, anxious. The wretched harridan should have been safely interred in the local churchyard by now.

The following Sunday dawned with sunshine glistening on a fresh fall of snow, bringing a bright blue glow to the windows. Bleakley dressed in his finest for church and walked into the kitchen to brew a pot of tea. Sarah was already there, sitting at the table. He flinched with shock as she raised her head and smiled. Her face was pale, the unnatural green-white of a glass of diluted absinthe. Her eyes glittered, bright with emerald fire. What he could see of her hair beneath her lace cap was also bright green ...Was this a side effect of the Scheele's dye?

'Husband … it is so very good to see you,' she murmured with a curious gaiety in her tone, 'and looking so handsome in your Sunday best.'

Sarah had never spoken in such a coquettish manner, even during their courtship.

'Come sit with me, my beloved …'

Whatever was wrong with his wife, she was far from being at death's door. She stood up and danced around the kitchen, her slim form if anything more petite, almost fey, moving with a sensuous grace he had thought impossible in one so repressed. She was not dressed to go to church; she was hardly dressed at all, wearing only her chemise, unbuttoned at the neck to reveal a pallid cleavage, and one petticoat, which she lifted in her dance revealing equally pale limbs.

To his horror, Sarah ceased her dance, sat on his knee and caressed his hair. Bleakley's skin crawled at the cold touch. Her fingers were like ice, like those of the dead. Yet there was nothing death-like about her animation and the predatory gleam in her eyes.

Horrified, Bleakley rushed for the door, slamming it behind him before fleeing to the sanctuary of the church. He sat in a pew at the back, ignoring the congregation and the fire-and-brimstone preacher. As he shook in uncontrollable fear, his mind raced with possibilities. Had the poisoned drink affected her mind and tinted her body? That pamphlet had spoken of the ill and often fatal effects of Scheele's Green. Perhaps he had not given her a strong enough dose to kill her outright? He had no choice but to return and finish the job. And find a way to disguise the ghastly colour of her hair and skin.

Too frightened to go home and face the horribly

transformed figure of his wife, Bleakley stayed in the church all day, sitting through service after service, his head buried in his hands. When Reverend Jackson approached, concerned, Bleakley spun a tale of needing a day of prayer, being so worried about his dear wife's poor health, cutting off all further enquiries by mentioning the taboo subject of 'feminine problems.'

Eventually there could be no more stalling. Gathering every inner resource of courage, Bleakley trudged back through the snow. Once at home, he found the house mercifully quiet. He went straight into his parlour and poured all of the last vial of dye into the absinthe.

Bleakley began to walk away from his misdeed when a swirl of cold air announced he was no longer alone. Heart hammering, he turned around to see Sarah yet more transformed. His body shook in terror. Whatever stood before him with an eerie attempt at a coquettish smile was not his wife. The unloved, unlamented spirit of Sarah Bleakley had departed this shell of flesh to her heavenly reward and whatever inhabited it now was not human.

Huge green eyes with the iridescent gleam of a cat's caught in lamplight fixed on the terrified man, draining his willpower and ability to flee. She was naked, her skin a corpse-pale, milky-green. Her hair worn loose was bright emerald, flowing and coiling around her face as if blown by some inner breeze. Too terrified to focus, Bleakley dimly thought he saw green wings spring from between her narrow shoulder blades, delicate, translucent as gossamer with green veins.

He knew he was now quite insane. The Green Fairy, *La Fee Verte*, could not really exist. She was an invention, the imagined wayward spirit of absinthe, no more. Maybe an inner, hidden guilt from poisoning Sarah had risen from his soul to punish him.

There was nothing imaginary about the entity's strength; Bleakley felt talon-tipped fingers dig deep into the flesh of his arms, hauling him over to his favourite chair, forcing him to sit down. The creature gave a graceful whirl of triumph before him, candle light illuminating an eerie green sparkle on her skin, like the light glowing from fireflies.

'Relax my beloved husband,' the creature crooned, in a voice far removed from Sarah's shrill whine. This was seductive, beguiling and chilling as the grave. She poured him a full measure of brandy and handed the balloon glass to him, forcing it into his reluctant, shaking hand.

'Let us drink a toast to new beginnings, my love.'

She took the poisoned absinthe and drank deeply straight from the bottle, before sitting opposite him, one leg cocked over the arm of the chair. An act so shameless, so wanton, Bleakley knew for certain no lingering trace of Sarah remained in this body. As he raised the glass to his face, he was hit by the smell of bitter almonds. He had a choice: drink the cyanide-laced brandy and die or live tormented by the Green Fairy.

Bleakley drained the glass. At least he would not meet Sarah again, not where his soul was destined for. God was merciful after all.

SHADOWS IN THE LIMELIGHT

A town in the Midlands, 1876

The discomfort from the rain did not bother Bernard Stubbins. He hurried through the emptying streets, oblivious to the rainwater seeping through the thin soles of his boots and past his starched collar down his neck. Soon he would be dry, warmed by hundreds of bodies around him, all transfixed by the limelights illuminating a wooden stage. The crowd would be excited, like him, by the variety show to come. The Great Rolando and His Merry Minstrels had come to their industrial town in the Midlands, a dour, grey place starved of colour and entertainment, and Stubbins was not going to let a mere downpour ruin his night out.

Stubbins pushed all dreary thoughts about his life and surroundings aside, even if only for a few cheery hours. Ahead he could see gilded light stream from the theatre entrance, dancing on the puddles outside like molten gold.

Hidden in the wings, the Great Rolando, born Eric Henry Jones from Penge, watched without satisfaction as the seats to the small theatre filled with another horde of grimy locals. More philistines and peasants to entertain; it was truly like throwing pearls before swine. He stood resplendent in his master of ceremonies garb: a shiny top hat and a bright red tail coat over a gold brocade waistcoat that strained to cover his pot belly. He projected a merry-hearted, avuncular figure to the audience, too far away to notice his mean little eyes like chips of black granite in an increasingly bloodshot setting.

A bitter, spiteful man, he was haunted by the relentless ghosts of his ambition and pride, his lost dreams of performing to the crowned heads of Europe. Not that it would show once he stepped on stage, the consummate professional. Rolando would wear his painted smile and his cloak of jollity and none of the audience would know how much he despised them.

His troupe were not so fortunate.

The woman who was once, briefly, a young girl called Meg Brown took in a deep intake of breath as her helper, Bizarro the Magician, pulled hard on her corset lacing. She was a fading soprano of undetermined age and increasing girth who lived and sang under the name Consuela, the Soprano of Seville. She actually came from Camberwell, but her dark looks and roughly approximate Mediterranean accent had never caused complaint. Nor had her voice, until recently, when a penchant for cheap gin and even cheaper Egyptian cigarettes had coarsened it and stolen her once pure top notes. Consuela doubted this crowd would notice, unlike the more discerning London audiences. At least it was many miles from their home theatre; somewhere different, somewhere safe.

The last nights at their permanent base in Hackney, The Rialto Theatre of Dreams, had been a nightmare. One of their best acts, a beautiful, talented ballerina, little more than a child in petite appearance, had disappeared without trace. Hitting the bottle hard, a surly Rolando had first told the troupe that Belinda had run away to be the spoilt plaything of some titled back-stage Johnny. Something Consuela had not believed for one minute. The dancer was too intelligent, too wise, to let her head be turned with flattery and the promise of money. Another night, he had slurred that the girl had been poached by a travelling circus to dance on horseback in the ring.

'Heartless little whore, dazzled by some showman's false gold,' a drunken Rolando had thundered backstage, barely able to stand up, let alone present that night's performance. 'Wait till she first falls on her backside in horse shit in front of the crowd, then she'll be back, begging.'

None of this made much sense to the rest of the cast, in particular Consuela, who had been a mother figure to the dancer and knew she had been happy and content staying with The Merry Minstrels. At the very least, Belinda would have found some way of saying goodbye. A scribbled note; a fleeting, tearful hug; a letter from her new life. Something. It didn't make sense. Nor did their boss's sudden decision to forgo their theatre to take the show on an impromptu tour of the country, after a day spent sending frantic telegrams. What did make sense to Consuela was getting away from the Rialto. Since Belinda's disappearance, the atmosphere had darkened; it had become a shadowed place of dread without obvious cause. Superstitious by nature, few of the performers mentioned it out loud for fear of jinxing the troupe, but many had seen a baleful and motionless grey shadow backstage. Consuela had seen it herself and could tell the others who had; she could see it in their eyes.

'Yer on in ten minutes,' rasped Roland. 'Bizzy, 'urry up and get that fat sow laced up, there's only so long this mob will be entertained by Fannie and 'er bloody dancing dogs.'

Bizzy gave the woman a comforting hug, disgusted by the coarse insults from their odious boss. He could see the hurt in Consuela's heavily made up eyes, the tears that threatened to streak the thick layers of greasepaint.

'We don't have to put up with all of this,' he murmured for the umpteenth time. 'We could break away, start a life of our own.'

Consuela finished dressing and gathering up her frayed dignity, turned to kiss him on the cheek. 'The show must go on, my sweetheart. We are nothing if not true professionals.'

What would she have done without her beloved Bizzy? If he had another name, no-one knew it. He was still a good-looking man, one who must have turned heads when younger, long before Consuela knew him. A man good on the inside too, which was a rarity in her world. Heart of gold, that was Bizarro, the not-very-competent magician. An early battle with opiates had robbed him of his once dextrous sleight of hand, skills in illusion that had once entertained high class audiences across Europe and Russia. Then he was The Astounding Bizarro. A title he had dropped himself when his props began to tumble onto the stage at the wrong moment and the audience's laughter grew cruel and derisory.

There was a story to tell about his past, Consuela was certain of that. His speech and genteel manners seemed aristocratic to the singer. She fantasised he was the wayward youngest son of nobility, the black sheep who preferred the glamour of the theatre to a predestined role in the clergy. He was once the boy who ran away to join the circus. This was all her wild imaginings of course. Bizzy could have just been the well brought up son of a respectable grocer, a lad born with an adventurous soul. She never pried; it was not the way of their kind. You could be whatever you wanted to be in their star-spangled world of illusion.

Illusion was all they had now. Consuela glanced into the cracked and grimy mirror and created an illusion in her mind that she was still 20, slim and beautiful. That there was no grey in her dark hair or deep wrinkles beneath the thick greasepaint. That her voice was as clear and true as cut crystal glass and the waiting audience would take her to their hearts.

What was wrong with this place? A minute ago, the tiny and pitiful excuse for a dressing room had been humid and stuffy, impossible to remain there for long before her greasepaint began to melt and her clothing dampen with unwanted perspiration. Now it was cold as a snow-covered grave. Consuela shuddered and reached back for her faded velvet cape, caught a shimmer of silent movement. From the corner of her tear-blurred eye, she saw a grey shadow form in the corner. Something still and not of this world.

No, not here! Not a hundred miles from their London base. She fled from the dusty store-cupboard that served as her dressing room, gathering up the many flounces of her bustled skirts to clatter in panic up to the stage wings. Fighting for calm and her breath, she was not even aware of the weak applause for poor old Fannie and her arthritic poodles. The boss was though. The show had only just started and the crowd were already bored and restive. It wouldn't be long before stinking old cabbages would litter the stage and threaten his performers with humiliation and injury. The first he wasn't bothered with, the second could threaten the takings if his acts couldn't perform.

Ignoring her wide, frightened eyes and face blanching despite the thick make-up, Rolando gave a tough shove and pushed the soprano to one side, 'The last thing this lot needs to see is another worn out old bat. Oi, Firebrand ... get out there. At least a bit of daredevil knife-juggling and fire-eating will shut 'em up.'

Consuela backed away from the wings, grateful Bizzy was not within earshot. One of these days, his patience and calm temperament would fail; he would snap at one of Rolando's endless insults towards her and murder the vile little bastard. Or better still make him disappear, unlike the white rabbits and playing cards that always showed up on stage at the wrong moment. At least that made the audience laugh. Such outlandish, wishful thoughts of Rolando's disappearance briefly shut out the fear of whatever lurked in the dressing room. Would it be still waiting there for her after she performed? Or had it moved on to haunt others in the troupe? Maybe Bizzy was right, and it was time to quit the Merry Minstrels and move on. This could be a sign.

The daredevil act was well-timed. The ripples of awe and animated gasps from the audience reached the waiting performers and soothed their nerves, even more so when Firebrand got demands for an encore. Leave 'em wanting more was Rolando's attitude, and he ushered his star performer from the stage, ignoring the boos and catcalls from rowdier elements in the crowd.

They were silenced by a loud crack as a bolt of lightning outside the theatre briefly seared eyes with its blue/white flash, startling everyone. Despite the crowd's uneasy noise, mainly were still fearful. A deep rumble of thunder rolled above the theatre, dark and dramatic in tone. Rolando laughed as nature added to the night's spectacle. The crowd would remember this long after forgetting the tattered garb and tarnished spangles of his performers. With no other choice, he beckoned to his soprano to get her fat backside on stage, angered by her hesitancy.

He was not to know that Consuela was terrified, not of the audience or the violence of the storm but of the grey, formless shadow that had left the dressing room and was now in the wings. It was something that did not belong here, could not belong here, and yet there it was. Mute and still and yet horrific, chilling her to the depths of her soul. What was it? Why did it haunt the company? She winced in pain as the master of ceremonies gripped her arm, dragging her from the wings and onto the stage to a reception of cat calls and whistles. Another thunderbolt exploded as if ripping open a wide fracture in the sky, releasing hellish horrors onto the Earth. This prompted a few startled shrieks from the women in the audience and some cussing of alarm from the men. The lightning had hit something in the town and it was too close for comfort.

Prompted by a furious glare from Rolando, the orchestra struck up an opening, familiar chord. Old instincts took over and Consuela began to sing, her voice just powerful enough to be heard above the thunder's doom-laden drum rumbles. At first the crowd were silenced by her courage and the beauty of her song, a skylark defying nature at its most powerful. But as she missed the first top note badly, the mood turned and booing joined the cacophony of sound. Could the evening get any worse? Consuela's instinct was to flee the stage, flee the grey shadow in the wings and bolt for an uncertain future, but her decades of professionalism took over and she continued to sing, waiting for the inevitable rain of debris onto the stage. The signs were there, many were now standing up, the better to propel rotten fruit and vegetables onto the stage.

It did not happen. A puzzled Consuela became aware of the crowd quietening and sitting back down in their chairs. As she sang on, the soprano realised their focus was not on her, but on something behind and around her, something that enthralled and enchanted them. Consuela dared not look around in case she broke the spell, but sang on. Miraculously her voice had cleared enough to hit the high notes, this time with the clarity of a heavenly bell tuned by angels. The crowds sighed with delight as her unseen accomplice shared the stage but never once impeded or blocked her from the crowd's view.

All she could sense was a brief cold draught as the stranger passed behind her, with no footfall or sound of breathing. Her thoughts racing, Consuela realised she was not afraid, that this mysterious entity meant her no harm but was helping her get through the performance … like in the past?

And then she knew who it was. What it was. No longer did she fear the grey shadow. It did not return from its unknown grave to haunt her. As the soprano finished her aria and took her bow, she was aware of the presence beside her. Consuela held out her hand and felt the lightest of touches, a spectral, almost child-like hand in hers. Together they acknowledged the cheers of an appreciative crowd.

The singer glanced to the wings, taking in the sweet scent of revenge. For Rolando had collapsed, eyes wide with terror, babbling incoherently to the cast who rallied to help him. A terror born of guilt. Consuela gave the ethereal hand of the young dancer a gentle squeeze. Together they would torment and avenge their mutual enemy, the vile and murderous Rolando.

The mill workman, Stubbins, waited until the final, jaunty note from the orchestra was played, the last performer had taken their bow, before leaving the theatre. Inside, as the crowds filed out, the limelights were extinguished and the magic faded into memories. And what memories he had. His mind still span with the glittery colours and spectacle. Outside, in the real world, the storm had passed, leaving the air fresh and cool, the streets washed clean of all ordure and debris. Lit by a near-full moon, the ground glistened as if brand new.

He took in a deep breath of the fresh night air after hours in close contact with the stench of other people, their sweat, alcohol, tobacco and tawdry perfume. Tonight would not improve when he arrived back at the cheap lodgings, the cramped room he shared with five fellow mill workers, with their snoring and malodorous body functions. But for now he was still lost in the illusion of glamour from the theatre, and most of all that wondrous dancer accompanying the singer. The sylph-like ballerina, with the sad, pale and so beautiful face, who danced with footsteps as silent and light as a butterfly, who could leap so high and soar as if borne aloft by invisible wings. It was as if she did not belong to this world, but was an ethereal being made from fairy dust.

Stubbins would never forget her fey beauty. He would hold her image in his heart, a special memory for when life's hard toil became too much too bear.

BREATH OF THE MESSENGER

A Lovecraftian Steampunk Tale

London, 1876

Jonas Fairfax ran, covering his mouth and nose with a woollen scarf that did little to keep out the foul miasma engulfing the city. But Fairfax didn't care. He just ran.

It had started with a normal occurrence, a thick, seasonal fog that often rose from the Thames to mix with industrial waste, household soot and the foul emissions belching from the Ephesysium Gas Works. A London Particular, the locals would call it. A pea-souper. Only Fairfax knew that this one was so much more, this Particular fog was tinged with a spreading and deadly malign effluence of occult origin.

Fairfax was the only living human to know this, now his master was dead by his own hand. And what kind of maniac cuts out his own heart with a kitchen knife? He had arrived at Vespasian's basement in Whitechapel a few minutes before, steeling himself to plead with the mage to stop his infernal experiment. It was too late. Fairfax found the old man covered in still steaming gore, lying on his back, his face contorted with terror and insanity. His right hand clutched a knife, his left gripped his heart. It was the expression on his master's face that caused Fairfax to flee in panic. What nightmare had he seen, to die so horribly by his own hand?

At first Fairfax had been content to go along with what he thought harmless eccentricity. He had been well paid by Vespasian; he doubted even a servant in the employ of Her Majesty could expect better remuneration. For an ex-thief with no trade, he had been content to seek out the obscure and arcane objects and potions Vespasian demanded. Even to the extent of using his criminal skills to acquire what he could not purchase.

It was all nonsense. Nothing would happen. Vespasian was senile, barely able to remember his own name. Even though Fairfax did have to accept that London had changed beyond all recognition when, decades before, another bumbling fool had opened a lower rung of Hell, releasing demonic vermin to plague them all. But London's citizens had learned to live with and avoid the parasitic Breeth and scavenging Blaggers. Fairfax doubted the old fool could raise more than a mild breeze in a teacup, never mind a storm. Contacting the Great Old Ones, whoever they were, would never happen.

But something *had* occurred. And it was enough to frighten Vespasian into a terrible death at his own palsy-trembling hand. Something that now filled the narrow, dark streets with a creeping, silent, choking dread. Fairfax ran from Whitechapel as if pursued by the Hounds of Hell. The miasma could be their vile breath for all he knew. At first his flight had no direction, no purpose beyond getting far away from that basement. As the polluted air forced its way into painful lungs, Fairfax slowed down, paused to rest against a dank inn wall reeking of stale urine, vomit and old, cheap beer.

His mind raced in time with his frantically beating heart. Where to go? What to do? Then, through his confusion, he remembered the tavern talk of a man who may be able to help, give him refuge. The notorious maverick, the alchemist Cyrus Darian: a ruthless bastard but one well versed in all supernatural matters. It was said he lived with a demon prince in human form. Another bonus. Surely a creature of such power would be able to protect him too?

Vexed, Cyrus Darian tapped the wooden floor of a steam Hansom with his cane topped with a crystal orb. Another night at the theatre ruined by the Particular. Damn this confounded atmosphere! He had looked forward to the performance of a much feted Italian songbird – the lovely Allegra. Even more to the prospect of an amorous liaison with her after the concert. His dark good looks and dangerous but alluring charisma meant he was rarely refused willing female company. But the wretched smog seeped through every opening to the theatre, filling it with foul, stinking air, and obliterated sight of the stage even with the limelights on full. As usual, it burnt people's throats, causing nausea and difficulty breathing. More wretched souls would meet their maker that night from the effects of the fog. And of course no singer would risk the precious gift of her voice in such circumstances.

With no other choice, Darian left the theatre

quickly at the first sight of the Particular, hailing a steam cab before they became scarce, and with the more-than-generous offer of a gold sovereign in payment, he bid the driver to take him to his Mayfair home.

As the vehicle chugged and wheezed its way from Drury Lane, Darian gazed out of the window and was puzzled by the nature of the fog. He had never seen one so dense. Indeed it appeared solid, such a strange dirty orange colour, and the smell … a fetid charnel house stench that made him gag with revulsion. No gas lamp could pierce the gloom, and the streets normally so busy at this time of night were emptying. He doubted even the most desperate streetwalker needing her supply of gin would be plying her trade that night.

As the journey progressed, Darian became aware of a growing unpleasant sensation, a soul-sapping depression of his spirits, a toxic combination of dread, fear and hopelessness. He forced it aside. It was not real, merely another effect of the still-thickening miasma.

He began to wonder, however, what was the nature of this occult assault and who was the perpetrator?

On arrival at the steps of his Georgian townhouse, Darian gave the driver the promised sovereign and hurried the short distance into his home. Even that was enough to confirm his belief that there was nothing natural about the fog. It was a warning, a portent of impending danger, that something bad was coming and the miasma was merely the beginning.

Darian found himself alone. His companion Belial had left on a mission of his own earlier that night, to prowl among the secret taverns frequented by demonic half-breeds to gather any information of use in acquiring interesting artefacts. And, of course, to indulge in some recreational unspeakable debauchery. For in his weakened human form, High Prince of Hell, Belial, had physical needs in which to indulge.

While he waited for the demon's return, Darian stoked up a hearty fire in the parlour and poured himself a large measure of fine old cognac. Rich as Croesus, the alchemist, hedonist, thief, philanderer, necromancer and compulsive liar no longer kept servants. Too many had been lost to his experiments when they went wrong or been caught in the crossfire when he was attacked by his many enemies. Lack of staff also gave Darian the freedom and secrecy to live his delightfully degenerate life to the full without the distraction of rumour and public censure.

He must have dozed off in the old leather armchair by the hearth, for when he awoke, stiff and cold, it was morning and the smell of freshly-brewed coffee rose from the kitchen. Darian stood up with a wince at his complaining muscles as he stretched. He followed the enticing aroma, finding Belial preparing breakfast for them both. The demon paused to pass a letter to Darian. The envelope was soaking wet and filthy with grime.

'Found this clutched in the hand of a corpse on your doorstep. I assumed it was for you.'

Darian took the letter, puzzled. 'And the body?'

'Disposed of,' Belial replied with a slight shrug. 'As always.'

A Fallen Angel, one of seven High Princes of Hell, on Earth Belial had taken the form of a slender youth, beautiful, with long, pale gold hair and amber eyes that reflected an ageless, corrupt evil. His devotion to Darian was unswerving, an obsessive fidelity that exposed the cruelty of his cursed existence. A doomed love that could never be fulfilled without an eternity of disaster befalling them both.

The alchemist studied the frantic scrawl of a terrified soul, one that knew his life was over. A plea for help that went out beyond the grave.

Darian glanced up at the demon. 'What knowledge have you of the Great Old Ones?'

Belial feigned a yawn of boredom. In truth he never tired, never needed to sleep.

'Luckily for you humans, they keep to their own dimension. They are vast, humourless, incredibly ugly bastards with a predilection for destroying whole planets on a whim. Usually when some fool summons them. They do not like their eternal sleep disturbed.'

Darian nodded. He had once read something similar in one of his Grimoires but had dismissed it as irrelevant old legends not based in reality. How wrong he had been.

'Well, my friend. Our unfortunate deceased visitor was trying to seek shelter from the results of his master's meddling with these Great Old Ones. I take it that is bad news?'

Belial stood up abruptly and paced over to the window. It was seven in the morning, but no sunlight could pierce the pall of smog that engulfed London, if not the whole country.

'The worst news possible. If that fool has indeed made contact, then all human life on this world is at peril. Does our visitor name the Elder God involved?'

Darian returned to the note, struggling to make out a name in the desperate scrawl. 'Yghraal?'

The demon gave a sigh. 'Then there is hope, a slight one. Yghraal is a celestial messenger. A go-between and not an actual god. He serves Pharol, a black-fanged, one-eyed demon who lives in a seething realm of chaos beyond this universe.'

Darian decided coffee was not enough in the circumstances and sought out an unopened bottle of brandy in a kitchen cupboard. After generously lacing both of their cups, he sought more information. 'So, why this Pharol? Why seek contact with something so horrendous, so destructive?'

'Vanity,' Belial answered. 'Vanity and greed. This fool must have learnt that another occultist did, in fact, successfully contact Pharol to gain arcane information to strengthen his occult abilities. A wizard called Eibon of Hyperborea. Only he was a powerful enough sorcerer to contact Pharol directly. This idiot has tried to engage an intermediary and thus doomed humanity.'

'And what happened to this Eibon?'

The demon gave a humourless grin. 'Nothing comes for free in this universe. But humans foolish enough to deal with us Fallen do have the hope of redemption and salvation. Unfortunately! No such good fortune with these Elder bastards. The man is languishing in agonizing perpetual torment on a distant world with no possibility of escape or death. Ever.'

Belial picked up his coffee and sipped it thoughtfully. 'Our biggest problem is dealing with Yghraal. He must be stopped before leaving this world. I know he is still on his way here because of the wretched miasma. It is the Breath of the Messenger. That which brings madness and death to all that inhale it.'

'Splendid.'

Darian did not hide the bitterness in his voice. He had saved England twice over the past year and not one citizen of this great empire would lift a hand to help him.

His half Persian, half Irish birth made him a despised outsider, a filthy, untrustworthy foreigner. Well, they had got the untrustworthy bit right. His refusal to accept the authority of the British establishment marked him as a maverick and pariah.

'Let someone else deal with it this time,' he announced. 'All those high and mighty generals and police chiefs. All the men of science with their open scorn for my alchemy and arcane learning. I've done more than enough.'

Darian picked up the brandy bottle and took a big swig. 'Let's wake up Hardwick and take his dirigible to somewhere with clean air and beautiful, willing women.'

'I am sorry my friend,' Belial answered. 'That will buy you only a week or two of freedom. Nothing will stop the spread of the Breath of the Messenger. It will engulf every country on the planet. I doubt if any human will survive.'

Darian learnt from the demon that the current smog was unpleasant and dangerous to those with weak lungs, but with Yghraal's arrival, it would strengthen to a poison infecting the brains of all living things, turning them suicidally insane. The uncharacteristic depression he had suffered in the Hansom was a mere foretaste of what was to come.

'Then we must still get to Hardwick. No doubt he has some respiratory devices I can utilise.'

The demon agreed but insisted on travelling alone to reach their companion in adventures, the aristocratic inventor and genius Sir Miles Hardwick. 'There is nothing these tiresome beings can do to harm me. But, my friend, you are *not* immune to the Breath. We must hope Miles can come up with a technological solution to this disaster. Your old earth magicks and weird potions will be useless.'

Glancing across to his companion, Darian looked for a glimmer of hope to pierce the spreading gloom. 'Come on, old chap, you are a High Prince of Hell! Are you telling me that you have no influence over this Yghraal?'

Belial did not answer, had no need to. In order to fight the Messenger, the alchemist must reverse the summoning, to return him to Hell and regain his full, awesome cosmic power. The chance of Lucifer and the other princes allowing him to return to Earth and save mankind was negligible, at the most optimistic. It would not happen.

So nothing more was said, the demon went to seek out Hardwick and Darian retreated to his library, seeking anything from ancient tomes that could aid their battle against Yghraal. Yet again it was down to him and his stalwart companions to set things right. How tiresome.

The alchemist lost all sense of time as he concentrated on translating ancient Sumerian and Chinese inscriptions, all to no avail. His futile search ended at the rhythmic thud, wheeze and huff of a steam-driven dirigible arriving at the mooring point above his home. The unmistakable sound of well-tuned and perfectly-engineered machinery: the *Dauntless* had arrived.

Shaken to the core, Hardwick hastily descended to meet the alchemist within the townhouse whilst Belial remained to check the dirigible's secure moorings. The Mayfair square was quiet. Empty. But Belial could sense the sounds of suffering in the distance. How he would have loved to join in the mayhem, glory in human pain and bloodshed, but his place was at Darian's side. He had to protect him against this spreading chaos.

'It's bad, Cyrus. Spreading like a nightmarish plague across the city. Fires, explosions … the screams …' Hardwick's hands shook, his face had a grey pallor. 'The terrible shrieks … London has become a charnel house of the damned.'

'Then we do not have much time to stop this,' Darian replied with a weary inevitability. 'What have you brought?'

'Respirators, obviously. They are frightfully heavy I am afraid, but they produce their own air supply rather than filtering the surrounding air. I assume you have an occult-based plan?'

Darian poured three glasses of cognac with a more than generous measure, and handed one to the inventor. 'Actually no. Not a thing. I was rather hoping you had a technological solution, old chap.'

Hardwick downed his cognac in one go. 'Then your fiendish playmate is right. Humanity is doomed.'

Materialising over London, a mountainous shape of roiling gases gathered strength, feeding off the agony rising from its victims, revelling in their pain and despair. In a mindless thrall to Vespasian's spell, one created with the spilled blood of a hundred innocents, it sucked everything into itself. It needed the energy of the humans' murderous, suicidal insanity, their last dying gasps to give it enough power to cross vast universes and traverse an infinity of dimensions in search of its master Pharol.

Beneath it, London's streets ran with hot, crimson rivulets, pooling into lakes of gore from those caught in the deadly miasma. Some killed in a blind rage, oblivious to the identity of their victims, before turning their ire on themselves. Fathers murdered sons. Neighbours turned on neighbours. Some blundered through the streets attacking anything living in their path, adding carriage horses and dogs to the growing death toll.

Approaching the baleful cause of the slaughter, the crew of the *Dauntless* were safe from succumbing to the madness due to the cumbersome but effective respirators. From his scientific viewpoint, Hardwick studied the gaseous monstrosity through a thermo-frigian telescope. Yghraal appeared to have no substance, though was clearly a sentient life form. A single red orb pulsated on a snaking pseudopod protuberance that he took to be an ocular structure.

A gaping maw surrounded by tendrils of waving cilia opened and Yghraal bellowed in grim triumph.

'Hang on, we're in danger,' Hardwick managed to cry as the shock waves from the creature's roar battered the dirigible. It was only Belial's demonic strength and quick reactions at the helm that prevented the airship from plunging to its doom as the strength of a full hurricane blasted at the vulnerable canopy. Buffeted, the *Dauntless* was thrown and spun like a leaf in a gale.

'Point her bow upwards,' Hardwick roared above the cacophony as he applied full steam power to the airship's engines. 'We must get her high, above and away from this bloody turbulence.'

The dirigible fought against all attempts to regain control. It was easier for her structure to give in to the power of the infernal blast – let it blow her canopy at will – but after minutes of desperation, the *Dauntless* returned to the control of her crew.

'That little display of ill-temper was for our

benefit,' Darian mused. 'It knows we are attempting to tackle it head on.'

'And failing in spectacular fashion,' muttered a despondent Hardwick, wiping his brow with an oil-stained kerchief.

Darian borrowed the enhanced telescope and studied their foe. 'Actually, I think not. If it tried to repel us, then it feels threatened by us. It is vulnerable.'

He handed the instrument back to Hardwick. 'Look within the miasma. Can you see the bolts of lightning? And occasional glimpses of a white-hot plasma at the thing's centre? There must be a heat source powering its existence.'

'For all its sound and fury, it is only a messenger to the Elder Gods,' agreed Belial. 'It may have an Achilles Heel, so to speak.'

Hardwick paced the dirigible's gondola, agile mind racing with this new information. From its appearance and violent discharges, the plasma looked electrical in origin. Could a reverse galvaniser driven deep into its heart and earthed to water perhaps discharge the power and defeat it?

'We need metal cable, a great deal of it. And enough courage to get as close as possible to that monstrosity.'

'Then I suggest we fly the *Dauntless* to the docklands,' Darian suggested. 'I cannot think of another suitable source for what we need. The courage I cannot guarantee though.'

Hours later, moored above Hardwick's workshops in a converted mews block, the inventor, aided by Darian, worked hard to prepare a device. Every door and window was barred and locked, the gas lamps turned down as low as possible and a watchful Belial stood guard. Outside, a medieval vision of damnation raged through every region of London. Some people survived, locked in basements and cellars, but many were dragged out onto the streets to be butchered by those crazed by Yghraal's toxic fumes. The afflicted formed loose gangs to rampage in a deranged frenzy. When they couldn't find victims they turned on each other. What had once been doctors, clergymen, costers and housewives had now become ravening beasts, leaving the streets strewn with torn bodies and whole districts ablaze.

The beast grew in strength as its malign miasma spread beyond central London and onwards to the suburbs and surrounding villages. The whole of England lay helpless in its path.

'It is rough, flawed and crude,' announced an exhausted Hardwick, 'but it only needs to work once.'

The device was a cigar-shaped torpedo of roughly-hammered copper, rigged to a small galvanic motor. 'There is enough fuel to propel it for 20 seconds,' Hardwick said, aware the others would understand the implications. 'Which means getting very close to the monstrosity.'

'Twenty seconds is a long time,' ventured Belial in a mocking drawl. 'Too long. And you are assuming that the physics of your world apply to this being from another dimension.'

Hardwick had never hated the demon as much as now. He turned on him, the inventor's normally placid nature erupting into fury. 'Has the great Prince of Hell got another solution? No? Then I suggest your infernal highness shuts his foul mouth.'

'Gentlemen, please,' an amused Darian soothed.

'We have a vast cloud of reeking unpleasantness to defeat, can we put the old scores on hold?'

Once again, the *Dauntless* took to the choking skies, the air so polluted by the Breath now, that no breeze buffeted her canopy. Instead she moved by steam power alone, her way barely lit by a large galvanic illumination device whose blue/white beam could not pierce the gloom. The fog seemed solid now, a death shroud thrown over a lost city. The creature, confident of its victory, had moved from the heart of London, seeking new concentrations of human misery.

Just two people crewed the *Dauntless*. A bitter, angry Hardwick facing death with the stoic courage bred into his aristocratic genes, and a seemingly indifferent Darian, unbothered by the demon's last minute defection. 'Belial cannot help his behaviour,' he said. 'He is a Fallen Angel cursed to revel in humanity's evil towards its fellows. I bear him no ill will.'

All thoughts were put aside as they approached the Messenger, all vision now limited to Hardwick's ingenious invention, the thermo-frigian telescope that cut through the dense toxic pall and showed Yghraal's blazing core as a beacon fluxing through the miasma of its malign breath. The two companions shook hands, then held each other, patting each other's backs in a brief, awkward embrace, accepting this could be their last adventure together. At least in this life.

Despite his slender frame, Darian was physically stronger than the inventor and he chose to handle the torpedo, while Hardwick steered the *Dauntless* toward the Messenger's heart. Pulsating with power, Yghraal's amorphous form surged slowly away from the stricken city, gathering more energy as it passed across humans poisoned by its breath. If it was aware of the approaching craft, it gave no sign. Its one gelatinous orb fixated on the far horizon and the teeming cities beyond. Darian started up the torpedo's motor and lowered it and the metal cable from the airship as Hardwick steered them on a headlong collision course with their foe. Armed only with their respirators against the Messenger's influence on their minds, they planned to fly close enough to swing the torpedo into the plasma core of the being. A desperate plan for desperate times.

As they neared, the waves of infecting insane rage and suicidal despair from the beast's breath began to seep through the mechanism of their respirators. Darian could hear the inventor sobbing; a soul-deep wail of abject despondency. Too arrogant and selfish to be so easily affected, he flung the tethered torpedo from the airship and pushed Hardwick away from the controls. The inventor's despair turned to murderous rage, but pre-empting an attack, Darian floored him with a well-aimed uppercut to the jaw and concentrated on taking the *Dauntless* into battle.

Flying virtually blind now, Darian hauled the airship left and right, avoiding the lashing arms of Yghraal's long, writhing pseudopodia of hate. Its glowing orb whipped round to view its enemy up close, filling the glass screen of the *Dauntless*, flooding the craft with a baleful light.

'Got your attention now, you ugly, big bag of stinking wind,' Darian laughed as he threw the tethered end of the cable from the airship, sending the torpedo into its target. The creature flinched, unused to any opposition, giving Darian enough time to swerve away and flee. In his mind, he saw the snaking cable touch the earth, the plasma heart discharge its energy and Yghraal disappear in an explosion of dissipated energy. But that didn't happen.

Darian turned the vessel around and, looking through the enhanced telescope, saw the ravening beast untouched and unharmed. He swore in his native Farsi. It was time to abandon England, seek distant shores and re-assess the situation. If need be, spend the last weeks of his life in a blaze of hedonistic abandon. His many-times sold and damned soul would spend long enough in Hell!

But Yghraal was not finished with the impudent vermin who dared oppose it. A lightning-swift tentacle lashed out from its body, hitting the *Dauntless* with the impact of a vast, cracking whip. The dirigible spun in a frenzy, its canopy losing inflation from the battering forces railed against it. With the ship's master still out cold, Darian did what he could to bring her down. A crash was inevitable: the best outcome was a survivable one. Using all his strength and quick-witted intelligence, the alchemist wrested a little power back to her failing engines and, with seconds to spare from disaster, found a passage through the wide boulevards near the Palace, bounced off the buildings lining Pall Mall before crash-landing in Green Park.

Badly bruised and head ringing from the impact, Darian pulled the inventor clear of his ruined airship and sought shelter in a nearby stand of trees. He expected the ship to explode into a fireball, but the *Dauntless* instead died with a whimper and one lone curl of black smoke. Even in its last moments, the dirigible was a lady. He lay, back resting against a tree, and watched the Messenger lumber towards victory against mankind through the glass of his respirator, determined to keep hold of his sanity for as long as possible.

His attention was caught by a billowing column of cloud approaching from the north. It swiftly became a vivid, ice-blue blizzard of cold light. As it neared, Darian could see many snowstorms swirl and clash within its form, striking blinding flashes of white lightning. These illuminated the roiling maelstroms of frigid power deep within the cloud. It formed itself into the shape of a striding cyanotic man. As tall as Yghraal, the man was now solidified into the form of blue ice. The chilling figure raised one fist and punched deep into the plasma heart of the cloud being. The Messenger's cilia-fringed maw opened into a vast, ragged abyss, letting out a deafening howl of outrage and pain.

The beast staggered backwards, its structure dissipating as tentacles of miasma broke away and dissolved. Fragments rained down on the streets below, splitting into myriads of worm-like creatures that sank beneath the surface in flight from their attacker. The colossal ice creature struck again, a glacial fury strengthening his blow, and Yghraal finally collapsed into oblivion, all traces of the poisonous fog gone.

The battle over, the victor transformed back into a mighty blizzard, then a cloud, before returning to whatever dimension he belonged to. Darian had but one thought … find Belial and thank him. He had never doubted the demon had left earlier not to revel in the carnage but to seek help. Belial's cursed devotion to him was too powerful to allow the alchemist to perish without a fight.

Darian waited until Hardwick recovered his senses and led the dazed man back through the ruined, blazing streets, past piles of corpses and the bewildered survivors stumbling like the living dead, wondering why their hands were covered in blood and gore. With no-one attempting to kill them, they arrived safely back at Darian's townhouse to find the demon waiting with a chilled bottle of vintage champagne and three glasses.

For the alchemist was right; Belial had not left his beloved Darian to gloat over the rioting inhabitants of a doomed London. Instead he had used his demonic power to summon the only approachable Great Old One, B'gnu-Thun, the soul-chilling ice god, gambling that the one thing these deities hated more than humans was each other.

'I doubted your brave plan would work, so I called up a favour,' Belial announced, holding up his champagne glass in a toast to himself. 'Great Old One up against a mere messenger made of filthy fog? It was no contest.'

Belial enjoyed the look of outrage on Hardwick's bruised face. 'I will have to torture and annihilate some unfortunate humanoids on another world sometime in the future in return, but that does sound rather splendid fun.'

Darian raised his glass toward the demon and smiled. 'On behalf of the no doubt ungrateful, wretched people of England, I thank you. But can we get the hell out of London for a while? It is going to be an utter bore while they clear up all this mess.'

He glanced across to the inventor, patted him on the shoulder. 'So sorry, old chap. We won't be able to travel in the *Dauntless*, a brave casualty in the battle.'

Hardwick pulled himself together. He was an English gentleman and he had no intention of running away from his damaged airship or the ruins of London's society. Unlike the louche, degenerate foreigner and his demon sidekick, Sir Miles Hardwick would use his ingenuity and hard work to rebuild the airship and help restore order to the city he loved. He told the others of his resolve.

'Well, see you in six months or so then,' Darian replied, turning his attention to the demon. 'So, where shall we go? You've made it impossible to go to Rome, Istanbul or Vienna, my short-tempered demonic friend. How about St Petersburg? Or Seville? I have the desire for the delightful company of a dark-eyed gypsy temptress or two.'

Belial gave his smile of eternally corrupted innocence. 'Make that three and you have a deal, Cyrus.'

AN MÁTHAIR GHRÁMHAR

Castlebar, Ireland, 1850

One by one the children filed in and took their places behind their allotted chairs. All were neatly attired, their pinafores white and starched, in stark contrast to the identical deep black of their garb. The two girls' hair was shining and pinned up, the three boys had faces pink from scrubbing with carbolic soap.

Their father, Henry Lloyd, entered the room and took his place at the head of the table and the family bowed their heads as he said grace. As ever, it was a bleak prayer of gratitude, laden with hidden threat of the dire consequences of wastefulness and greed – as if they needed this constant reminder. The stench of death clawed at every locked window of Killala House, seeping beneath any gaps in doorways, a full brutal assault when the main doors were opened.

Lloyd gave the signal to be seated and his family obeyed in silence. Austere in countenance, heart frozen in unexpressed grief, Lloyd was proud of his children and their handling of their mother's recent death during childbirth. He expected no hysteria, no maudlin tears or sentimentality from them, especially not in front of the servants. This blighted island was burying its dead in large communal pits; few were left with the strength to dig individual graves. The emaciated bodies of whole families had been thrown into limed holes in the ground like rubbish into a midden. How could their own sad loss be treated as anything greater than the suffering beyond the tall, iron gates of Killala House? Lloyd was grateful that his children understood.

That he had loved his wife, no man could question. He had devoted his life to her and their cherished children. Even as her precious life ebbed away in a flood of red, she still gave him one more gift of life, one more perfect child, a boy. From that terrible night on, Lloyd banned all traces of red from the house … nothing of that accursed colour could remain, no hair ribbons or the bold uniforms of toy soldiers, no furnishings or portraits containing red. The house seemed drained of all colour now, as if a mourning grey mist had fallen on every surface, permeated every room.

Another pall lay across all Ireland, the weight of suffering and sorrow mingled with smoke from blazing homes torched as yet more starving families were evicted, unable to pay rent on their hovels. Lloyd kept his family insulated from the daily toll of horrors behind Killala's stout walls, but they were not immune from their own personal tragedy. All laughter had ceased here and he doubted it would ever be heard again.

A maid brought in the family's dinner, a dull but wholesome broth of salted beef and onions, and they sat in silence as every morsel was eaten, the bowls scraped clean. They were the lucky ones; they were landed gentry. English Protestants blessed by their god not to starve in the Great Hunger, *an Gorta Mór.*

Living through this endless hell in near isolation, Lloyd had a clear conscience. He did not own land nor was he in a position of power. Killala House was his only inheritance as the youngest of an Earl's five sons. It had no tenants, no farmland or large sporting estate, not even surrounding parkland. He lived on a limited allowance, had given what he could to ease the famine- and disease-stricken locals, employed as many with large families as he could financially support.

Yet the skeletal, pitiless spectres of famine and pestilence stalked the land. No county was spared, especially Mayo, decimated by cruel evictions and death. Thoughts of fleeing Mayo with his children plagued him daily and kept him awake at night, but this had been Eliza's home. All their children were born here. Running away seemed an act of cowardice, one perpetrated by so many of the ruling class. Many landowners had never even set foot on Irish soil, employing brutal and heartless rent-collectors to bring a broken people further to their knees. He would not show such weakness, such vile lack of sympathy with the native Irish.

The loud cry of an infant broke his sombre chain of thought, the healthy sound of his son, Henry, awakening. He paused, listening, then relaxed reassured as he heard the sound of hasty footsteps on the stairs, and his son's silence as the nursemaid reached him with milk and comfort.

Rebecca gently took the hands of the two youngest children and helped them back up the stairs to the spacious and warm nursery, their refuge from the horrors of daily life that no locked gate could hide. As the eldest at 13, she considered herself nearly a woman now. She had helped Mama with her brothers and sisters when she was alive, now Rebecca had to step in and do more. It was expected of her and she didn't shirk from her responsibility, especially now Moira the nursery maid had little Henry to care for.

The girl was old enough to remember the happy times in this old house, a graceless square of green/grey stone stubbornly holding out against the strong winds and rain straight off the Atlantic. A storm that had probably started as a sea breeze of the coast of America and whipped up into a frenzy by its crossing of the turbulent ocean. She remembered a lost time of laughter and games, when her father would pick them up high off the ground and whirl them around in giddy joy. She recalled proudly riding her chestnut pony at the side of his hunter as they hacked together around the country lanes surrounding the town of Castlebar.

Then came the worried whispers among the adults, cutting off whenever she approached. The rides out stopped. Playtime was curtailed to only the walled kitchen garden. Visits to the town ended and the family had not left their home for three years, living in a claustrophobic world of their own. One that turned even more into itself at the loss of their beloved mother.

One by one the children, full of the dull but substantial broth, grew heavy-lidded, ready for bed. Rebecca made sure they were washed and dressed in their nightclothes, kissed and tucked up for the night. All the candles were extinguished and the nursery lit only by the glowing embers in the hearth, a warm and comforting dancing light. She couldn't sleep, her young mind haunted by the horrid incident earlier that day …

The children were playing in the walled kitchen garden, wrapped up warm, their breath like baby dragons in the frosty air. They had not laughed since losing Mama and were still not ready despite the resilience of their young age, but they ran and skipped, spun tops and chased hoops in celebration of freedom from the darkened silence of the house in this time of deep mourning

Scuffling between the children's legs and chasing any thrown object, Rebecca's little pug was the only light-hearted creature in the garden, but he was also an adventurous one. As the nursemaid entered to usher the children back into the house for supper, the dog slipped past her and ran to the front of the house. Forgetting this area was forbidden to the children, Rebecca ran in pursuit, calling out his name. But Toby was lost in his own canine adventure, his small legs blurring in full flight. Rebecca found him yapping furiously, his fawn back bristling at three figures gathered on the other side of the front gate.

Rebecca walked over to the defensive dog and scooped him up in her arms, mumbling her apologies at his rudeness. Her heart froze for several beats as she glanced up and saw the visitors properly for the first time. At first she thought they were corpses, skeletons draped in tattered, filthy rags that flapped in the ice wind. It was only when one of them looked directly at her, with glazed eyes set in well-deep dark hollows, that Rebecca realised these people were alive. It was a woman, impossible to age with her extreme emaciation. A teenage girl stood protectively by her side and a little boy, wizened with starvation, peered from behind what was left of her skirts. They were all bare-footed, their stick-like limbs caked with mud and dried blood.

Overcome with shock, Rebecca did not hear her father's swift approach until she felt his arms pull her close to his side. He walked over to the landless, starving peasants and, handing them money, wished them luck in broken Irish. Weeping with pity, Rebecca removed her hat, scarf, winter coat and gloves and passed them through the fence to the pitiful family. Her father nodded in approval and gave away his own gloves, warm woollen cloak and scarf before taking Rebecca back to the house.

'There must be more we can do,' she pleaded. 'We have so much compared with them.'

Lloyd sighed, proud of her compassion, frustrated at his helplessness.

'My dearest, precious child. I have already done much and will continue to do more to help these poor wretches. But I am but one man and have a large family to keep safe and fed. Even if I gave away everything I owned, the nightmare of the Great Hunger would still remain. I am so sorry.'

Now, in the quiet of their nursery, Rebecca could not keep that family out of her mind, a family too exhausted and weak to speak or even hold out their hands for help. They had just stood, defeated by the cruelty of their life, at the locked gates to a world they could never imagine. A world of warm beds and plentiful food. Where even Lloyd's horses and ponies had deep banks of clean straw to lie in and plentiful grain to eat. She prayed to a god she had given up believing in, hoping her small donation of clothing could help them get through another cold night in the open.

Eventually a fretful sleep overcame her thoughts; one that was soon disturbed by Henry crying in the baby's room next door where Moira slept next to his cot. He was not settling, his cries unnoticed. Where was the maid? She was taking a long time to fetch his milk from the kitchen. Rebecca pulled on her dressing gown as his cries became louder and increasingly distressed, but as she made her way to her new brother's room, she heard the lilting sound of a lullaby. The baby quietened at the sound, a soothing song in Irish. Rebecca could not remember the nursery maid singing in her native tongue before but was reassured the baby was being cared for. She returned to her own bed and this time, mercifully, a deep, dreamless sleep.

In the morning, as Rebecca helped the maid get the children up and ready for their breakfast and morning lessons, she asked Moira about the lullaby.

'Sing that lovely song again, Moira. The one that got the baby back to sleep last night. I'd love to know what the words meant.'

The maid's broad face crumpled into puzzlement. 'Sure I do not know what you mean, Miss Becky. The babby slept through the night without stirring, Lord bless his innocent wee soul.'

'But you must have!' Rebecca said. 'I heard you singing a sweet lullaby in Irish.'

Moira crossed herself and kissed the silver medal of the Blessed Virgin she wore on a chain around her neck, one she insisted had been blessed by the Pope in Rome. She walked away from Rebecca, busying herself picking up discarded clothing and toys from the floor.

'Irish is only for the poor and miserable peasants, missy. I do not speak it let alone sing in that primitive tongue.'

Rebecca sensed her discomfort was from fear rather than offence as the maid continued, 'A dream. That is all it was. A bad dream brought on by your encounter with those people at the gate. The nerve of them! Bothering gentle folk with their misfortune.'

The girl did not mention it to Moira again. Thinking it was all just a dream was the safest option. What else could it be? Despite the warmth from the morning fire, Rebecca shivered. After breakfast, she looked after the baby for a while, needing her own reassurance all was well with him. She buried her nose in the soft down of his blond hair, loving the sweet baby scent, the funny little sounds he made and the way his tiny fingers curled around hers. Tears ran down her cheeks. Her mother should be here doing this. If there was a god, Rebecca hated him. Hated him for taking away her mother, hated him for not protecting the people of Ireland whose devotion to their deity could never be questioned.

Unwillingly, her mind went back to an earlier nursery maid, when there was just her, Thomas and Geoffrey. An elderly woman, loving enough to the children but given to telling old tales from the legends of her people at bedtime. Scary stories to the little ones, of Irish ghosts, *Ban Sidhe* and the *Tais*. The woman was dismissed by her shocked employers when they discovered the stories gave the children nightmares, causing them to wake up weeping loudly in distress. Rebecca had not given old Emer a single thought until now. The memories did nothing to improve her unsettled mood.

That morning, her father seemed more preoccupied than normal, or at least what passed for normal since losing her mother. Rebecca helped him with the little ones' lessons until the special time when she studied more advanced subjects alone with him. Today he sat her before the fire and gave her a new book to study, a dry-as-dust account of Roman history, while he sat opposite, in near silence, gazing into the hearth as if mesmerised by the dancing flames. Rebecca wondered if his introspective mood had been prompted by the correspondence he had received from London that morning. She wished he would share his concerns with her. She was no longer just a child.

Lessons over, the dour weather had cleared enough for play, but Rebecca could find no relaxation in the kitchen garden. Throwing a ball for her dog became a mechanical reaction to his keenness. Her mind was too haunted by the family at the gate. Had their meagre gifts of money and warm clothes helped them at all? Were they still alive?

As the evening drew close, the clouds once again low and leaden, Rebecca realised she was dreading the night, fearful of hearing the Irish lullaby again. Entering her baby brother's room, she shivered. The temperature seemed much lower than in the rest of the nursery. But there was a well-stocked fire in the grate and the curtains were drawn against any draught from the stiff westerly breeze and lashing rain outside. Maybe the raindrops were tears for Ireland, for after three years of famine there were no human ones left to shed.

There were two new additions to the bedroom. Above Henry's cot was a wooden crucifix and on the nearby bedside table was a statue of the Blessed Virgin cradling the baby Jesus. These things had no place in the faith of her upbringing. They were symbols that seemed almost pagan in their importance to the native people. Yet Rebecca felt strangely comforted by them. No doubt they had been brought by Moira after that talk of the lullaby. She reached out and touched the painted plaster statue, liking the rich celestial blue of the Virgin's cloak and the pink roses by her bare feet. Her bright-cheeked face was delicate, beautiful, a sweet expression of love for the Holy Infant. Rebecca whispered a supplication

'Look after my little brother, Lady. Please give him your protection.'

As the nursery lights were extinguished, Rebecca was unable to settle, listening for anything amiss in the baby's room. Even knowing Moira had also gone to bed and was close to the child did not ease Rebecca's anxiety. She heard the steady rhythm of the baby's cradle rocking, his contented gurgles, then the silence of an infant's deep slumber. Her own sleep crept up on her, and when she awoke the morning sun had already graced the nursery. Moira sat on her favourite rocking chair by the hearth with little Henry happily babbling on her knee and waving his tiny fists at sunbeams.

Rebecca's anxiety eased a little; maybe the religious items had kept whatever it was from nearing the baby during the night. Perhaps the eerie lullaby would never be heard again. During the morning, she noticed her father's quiet, distracted mood persisted. Her lessons with him were little more than a reading session with a few questions at the end. The afternoon brought drama. The morning's sun had yielded to a blanket of low, yellow clouds and an oppressive, heavy atmosphere lowered cross the landscape, presaging an approaching Atlantic storm.

With the children confined to the house, her father had visited their rooms to spend play time with them and the baby. He had discovered the Catholic items above and beside the cot and removed them, to Moira's anguish and loud laments.

'Your faith is your own, O'Hare,' he had thundered at the woman, 'but it is not of this family. I will not have these relics of medieval superstition displayed around my children.'

Rebecca's eyes widened in alarm and met Moira's in a moment of mutual understanding. The woman knew something. Why else would she have put them there after the girl's talk of a ghostly lullaby? She watched in frustrated silence as Moira took the items from her master with an apologetic bow and bustled out of the nursery. Inside, Rebecca wanted to scream, 'No ... don't take them away, say something, Moira. Please ...' But, despite her desire to be considered a grown-up, at that moment she was just a child. Any talk of ghosts in front of her father and the poor woman would be instantly dismissed like old Emer Dillon before. Rebecca needed to speak to the maid alone, she had to know more, anything to keep little Henry's safe.

Clearly that was the last thing on Moira's mind. For the rest of the early evening, the maid kept herself busy, always surrounding herself with the younger children, making sure she was never alone with Rebecca. Her normally easy manner and ready smile were forced, her actions distracted and perfunctory. This did not go unnoticed by her charges. The children became fractious and unsettled. A situation made worse by the oppressive atmosphere fallen across the land, which darkened with an unnatural gloom.

Outside, after hours of brewing along the horizon, the storm finally erupted with unearthly fury, lashing Killala House's sober walls with stinging hail. The glowering sky went purple and was rent with blinding flashes. The children were fearful at each crack of piercing light, each deep, dark rumble of thunder, not helped by the distressed whimpers of their two little dogs cowering beneath the beds.

Moira gathered the children around the fire, and as she cradled the mercifully slumbering baby, with

Rebecca turning the pages and showing them pictures, she read them jolly stories, and not a doom-laden Irish one amongst them.

The door opened and their father entered followed by two of the kitchen staff bearing trays laden with a feast of small cakes, sweet biscuits still warm from the oven and mugs of hot chocolate. Lloyd bid the staff stay and join in, and soon the nursery became host to a party, a little enclave against the battering storm and the cruelty stalking the land. Rebecca felt a glow of love build within her, for her family and for her mother, for surely she was there too. She could almost feel her touch, pick up her scent of gardenias. Her father glanced across the heads of the others and gave Rebecca a smile, the first since their bereavement that had held genuine warmth and optimism. Maybe he felt it too.

'I have an announcement,' said Lloyd. 'For all of you, household staff and their families included. Yesterday I received a letter from your dear mother's beloved cousin, Edgar Turnbull. He has a fine house in Dorset that he has no use for. One with a small but productive farm with no current tenant. He proposed we take it as a gift in dear Eliza's memory.'

Most were too young to understand, but Rebecca and the older boys did. The lads looked ready to protest, while she gave a whimper of relief.

'It means we will be leaving Ireland, maybe not forever but for now. It's my fervent wish that my loyal Irish staff and their families should consider coming with us.'

A chance to escape the Great Hunger? Rebecca doubted any would refuse. Her father cleared his throat and spoke again.

'Confinement in this house has been so hard on

you, my beloved children. By trying to keep you safe I have made a prison. I wanted to remain, to be near Eliza in this our home, but I know now she will always be with us, wherever we live. She is in my heart and I can see her in all of you. I know your beloved mother loves you all and wants you to be happy. We cannot be happy here. Not now.'

As the last of the thunder grumbled its way towards Castlerea and the rain became a soft patter against the windows, Rebecca felt a subtle change in the nursery. It seemed colder, with a moving grey shadow barely glimpsed from the corner of her eye. She spun around. Nothing was there, but to her distress the sense of something wrong, something unwanted, remained in the room.

'We will begin to pack up our things in the morning. Ready to start a new life in Sidmouth.'

'Is that by the sea, Father?' questioned Thomas.

Their father stood up and smiled again. 'Indeed it is, clever boy. There will be sandy beaches with rock pools to explore and ice cream in the summer!'

Was it Rebecca's imagination or did she hear a loud, anguished sigh behind her at her father's latest announcement? And the sound of something breaking in Henry's room? No-one reacted to these noises, perhaps too caught up in her father's unexpected announcement. But the dogs heard something, something that caused them to cower and whimper, scrabbling frantically at the nursery door to be let out. As a maid opened the door for the pugs to escape, the sound of frantic whining and caterwauling rose from downstairs. Lloyd strode to the top of the stairs to witness the pugs joining his own dog, a golden retriever, and his late wife's two Persian cats in a state of total panic. The growling dogs, with their hackles raised, clawed at the front door, tearing at the wooden frame with their teeth to get out. The two cats, their ears flat against their heads, eyes black with fear, looked back up the stairs, and their backs arched as they hissed and spat at some unseen fright.

'What in damnation has gotten into those animals?' Lloyd queried aloud, visibly shaken. 'The storm has passed now.'

Back in the nursery, Rebecca was startled by the appearance of a grey shadow moving among the people there. How could they not see it ? To her astonishment, none seemed to notice it but she. Horrified, she watched it move from the far corner of the nursery and approach the group of children and adults enjoying the impromptu tea party. Her father's reappearance into the children's room made no difference to its stealthy approach. Rebecca wanted to point at it and shout a warning but fear froze the sound in her throat.

She saw it loom above Ellen, a nebulous grey shape at first, transforming into the spectral form of a gaunt woman. Empty eye sockets in a skeletal face, a stooping figure draped in a filthy, ragged shroud that ended in a trailing mist just above the ground. The danger shook Rebecca out of her state of fugue. She screamed, pointing to the horrific form, causing pandemonium among her family and servants.

Moira ran to the girl, holding her tightly. 'Hush now, Miss Becky, you are frightening the little ones, there's nothing to be afeard of ...'

The shrouded figure, mouth agape in a silent scream had glided over to Daniel, holding out its bony fingers above his head as if in a blessing ... or a curse. Rebecca became hysterical.

'Can't you see it! A ghost or something above your

head, Daniel!'

This was too much for her father, who grabbed hold of her arm and dragged her out of the room, away from the screaming children.

'If this is a foolish game, Rebecca, it is not an amusing one. What has gotten into you? You are normally such a sensible young lady.'

Weeping, Rebecca dropped to the floor, wrapped her arms around herself and began to rock backwards and forwards.

'I saw it, Papa. Heard it too, singing a lullaby in Irish over Henry's cot.'

'Who has been filling your head with this superstitious nonsense? Moira? Or one of the other servants?'

The girl's wretchedness over not being believed deepened her anguished sobs. 'No, Papa ... not one of them. I know what I saw, what I heard.'

'It is the *fear gorta*, a spirit of famine who rose from the Hungry Grass, the *féar gortach*.'

Rebecca and her father turned and stared at old Mrs Mackey, the family cook since the Lloyds' arrival at Killala. She ignored the fury on her master's face as she continued.

'Do not blame the girl, sir. 'Tis not her fault she has the Sight.'

Lloyd paced the floor. 'I am regretting ever employing native Irish staff. This is not the first time my children have been terrified by this scourge, this pagan darkness infecting this blighted island.'

Rebecca rose to her feet, wiped away her tears and faced her father, finding the strength to stand up to him.

'It was not the servants, Papa. Not one of them. Not even old Emer. I know what I have seen and heard.

To deny it would be to lie to you, and I have never done that. Or to Mama.'

The old woman pointed down to the still frenzied pets in the foyer.

'If you will not believe your daughter, Master, will you not heed the poor, wee animals? Surely they know there is wrongness in the house.'

Before Lloyd could answer, a shrill keening rose from the nursery, an unearthly sound that nothing living could create. White-faced, the man pushed Rebecca into Mrs Mackey's comforting embrace and stormed back into the nursery into the path of a whirlwind. A nebulous form blasted around the family in a tight, threatening orbit, wailing its deafening cry of ancient grief and eternal pain. The servants held the terrified children close, doing their best to shield them from the sight and sound of their ghostly assailant.

'What does it want?' Lloyd yelled back to the cook, who was still holding Rebecca in the hallway. 'How do I stop it?'

'It is ageless, sir. A spectre made from every famine that has befallen Eire. For this is not the first to have taken so many lives. It is also known as *An Máthair Ghrámhar*, the loving mother, eternally seeking her lost children. Collecting the souls of children with no-one to mourn them.'

'Well it is not having my children. My still-living and much-loved children. Do you hear that, creature? Be gone, damn you. There is nothing for you here!'

Lloyd stood his ground despite the creature buffeting him, striking at him with long talon-like fingernails. Phantom it may be, but it could draw blood. Soon

Lloyd's face and hands were ripped and gashed by the attacks. He did not see his eldest daughter enter the room and calmly walk to confront the creature, holding up her hands as if to stop it in its furious whirl.

Transfixed, Lloyd and the others watched as the girl stood her ground as the ghost halted and became the solid form of the emaciated, hollow-eyed woman at Killala's gates. The one they had helped with money and clothing.

'The *Fear Gorta* does not harm those that have aided it in human form,' whispered Mrs Mackey. 'Was there not tell amongst the staff of a peasant woman at your gates, Sir? One with children?'

'There was,' Lloyd answered, desperate to interfere and protect his daughter yet aware that in whatever way she was communicating with the spectre, it had quietened its furious attack and backed away. As he watched helpless in the face of the supernatural, Rebecca's body began to glow with a gentle warm light, a golden glow as if from many candles. The light grew stronger and spread out to encompass all the other children.

An intense wail of sorrow built up within the spectre, a keening sound that rose in volume until everyone was forced to clamp their hands to their tortured ears. Then it was gone.

Like a marionette whose strings have been cut, Rebecca fell to the nursery floor and lay still, as if lifeless. Horrified, her father reached her first, cradling her in his arms. Her face was white, bloodless, her body stiff and icy, and she seemed to have stopped breathing. Then Rebecca took a deep gulping breath and came to, her eyes wide and startled.

'I cannot see her now. Has she gone?'

Lloyd nodded through his tears of relief.

'Yes my beloved child, the evil spectre has disappeared.'

'I meant Mama. She told me what to say to the Hunger Woman. Gave me the light to send her away.'

Lloyd sent the children and their servants ahead of him to their new home in England. He remained behind to close up the house, distributing all he could to the local poor. At last he was ready to leave Ireland, his emotions in turmoil. Killala had seen his greatest happiness and deepest grief. As his carriage rattled through the main gates for the last time, he spotted three figures gazing out of the nursery window. The *Fear Gorta* and beside her, the teenage girl, the little boy. His eyes widened with bewilderment as more spectral faces appeared in every window of the house, a countless throng of ghostly children, many holding spectral infants and newborns.

As the carriage took off at a brisk trot away from Killala, Lloyd could see a curious, dense grey mist surrounding the grounds, a pulsing miasma that revealed itself to be the spectral forms of so many more dead children. The lost ones of this and every Irish famine, their number beyond counting, drawn from across time and every county in Ireland to be with *An Máthair Ghrámhar*, a loving mother.

A tearful Lloyd looked away, heart leaden with guilt and remorse, for he was part of the system that had created this latest, most terrible of disasters to befall this land. The house and wealth he enjoyed had been bought by the toil of a conquered, voiceless people, now on their knees from starvation and disease.

Had he and Rebecca not shown that pitiful, meagre amount of sympathy to the creature when she came calling at the gates, perhaps the outcome would have been yet more horrific ... that his own children could now be gazing out of the windows of Killala with dark shadows in place of eyes.

All he could do was flee to the safety of England, but he would not sell Killala: *Máthair Ghrámhar* could have that. For her family of ghosts.

A FATEFUL ENCOUNTER

**(Extract from *Cyrus Darian and the Technomicron*,
Steampunk Novel of the Year, 2011)**

London, 1864

It had to be here. Just had to be! He had followed every clue, spent much time in the unsavoury company of London's criminal underworld, even more with its supernatural denizens. All leading up to this appointment with a female fae in a basement beneath a row of ruins in Southwark.

Cyrus Darian, aged 25, alchemist, amateur dabbler in the occult, collector of antiquities and murderer, hesitated. Before him, lit by one flickering candle, was a stone step glazed with green algae slime, one of many that would take him far down below the city, away from the safety of a crowded street, the everyday bustle of people going about their daily business. One loud shout away from help.

He was alone: the writer of the message on the scrap of torn parchment stuffed under his hotel door had insisted. If he wanted possession of the Sumerian lifestone, he had to come here alone. That was not difficult. Since moving to London, Darian had made no friends; all of his acquaintances were as treacherous and untrustworthy as he was.

His heart hammering loud enough to wake the dead floating in the many underground rivers beneath the city, Darian tightly wound up a Luxis device and was rewarded by a beam of soft light. Modern technology triumphed over the candle's fragile glow. Instinct told him this choice of meeting place was not right, that no fae would ever dream of meeting so deep beneath the city with the weight of dead stone pressing down on the hidden earth. But desperation drove reason from Darian's mind. This was the last object he needed, the one thing that could help him defy every rule of the universe, to undo what could not be undone.

Ignoring the stench of stagnant water and the claustrophobia, he descended, every sense alert for danger. Known for their disdain of humans, the fae, though not malicious by nature, could lead people into danger through their indifference to the consequences to mere mortals. Despite his quick wits and courage, that included mere mortals such as Darian.

At the base of the steps, he raised the Luxis by its polished wood handle and swept the wan light around, illuminating a series of narrow corridors around a circular central hub. It was no more mysterious than an abandoned icehouse, one no doubt belonging to a grand mansion, now demolished.

Dozens of fat rats scuttled away from the beam. Darian exhaled with relief … no unnatural vermin … so far …

In fact there was nothing and no sign that anybody or anything had entered these chambers for some time. The coating of algae on the flagstone floor had no footprints beyond the trails of busy rats. He turned to leave and noticed something nailed to the wall close to the stairs. It was a metal key along with a scroll of parchment with a few words scrawled in a shaky hand.

'I admire the brave and the bold ... You came here alone and therefore, Mr Darian, you have passed my test. Here is the address and key to my home in Mayfair. What you seek and far more is waiting for you there.'

Cursing, Darian left the icehouse, furious at the slimy green mess on his shoes. What if this was someone's idea of a prank ... or worse a trap? He considered abandoning the search for the fae female but yet ... with the lifestone so close ... still within reach ... He couldn't resist the challenge. Even if it was a trap.

The address turned out to be a fine, tall Georgian townhouse overlooking a neat and prettily planted garden square. With the key in his possession, Darian expected no staff in attendance and let himself in.

He was immediately surrounded by the soft aroma of meadow flowers ... the signature scent of a fae. He put down his gloves and crystal-topped ebony cane and followed the trail of perfume, taking him up the elegant curve of the stairs and onwards towards the inevitable bedchambers. Darian grinned. His dark good looks enthralled and repelled females of many species with equal passion; why not this fae? He was led to an open door and he approached, cautious, aware but with growing excitement. Could the lifestone really be so close? Could the frustrations of false leads and the pursuit of fakes be finally over?

He stepped inside the chamber, a bright, feminine room, delicately decorated with taste and decorum. Less decorous was the fae female. A petite yet voluptuous form, she lay on the bed clad only in a wisp of silver gossamer voile. A magnificent mane of golden hair framed her elfin face, illuminated by huge green/gold eyes, cold but beautiful in a way only those of the magical fae race could ever be.

'My brave human adventurer … shall we celebrate the success of our business deal with some shared pleasure?'

Darian scanned the room for signs of treachery but saw and heard nothing untoward. He had never bedded a fae before and a dangerous curiosity began to take over his mind. But not completely. 'First, let me see the stone and then I will be at your fullest disposal.'

'Ah, Cyrus … you disappoint me … business first?'

The fae sighed and reached over to a bedside table, removing a red velvet pouch from a drawer. She took out what looked like a piece of dull basalt and handed it to Darian.

His hand shook at he cradled the lifestone, immediately realising it was genuine. It had an inner pulse, a heartbeat, steady and eternal. His mind reeled at what this deceptively simple thing could do … It could break the laws of the universe, shatter that which could not be broken …

Forgetting the fae female in his joy, even for a few seconds as he held the stone, was a serious mistake. One small hand reached over and caressed his face, the other stroked his inner thigh but Darian's mind was too full of what this stone could do once added to his other treasures. Absentmindedly he brushed her hand away.

'Give it back to me!' the fae's voice was strident … too strident. He spotted a large cut crystal bottle of French perfume on the bedside table. This was puzzling: fae had no need of artificial fragrance. Recovering from his surprise at her change in attitude, Darian apologised profusely and tried to summon up the enthusiasm to entertain the now furious female.

'We had a deal, Eliana … I kept my side of the bargain and will happily join you in an amorous celebration.'

The fae grabbed back the stone and threw him onto the bed. This was wrong … very wrong. The fae were not that strong. The scent of flowers had gone and in its place something earthy and fetid permeated the air. It was a sickening aroma. She pinned him down, clawing and tearing off his clothing, the coldly beautiful eyes becoming harder, more yellow than gold. As she straddled Darian, he could feel the soft fae skin become coarse. He swore and struggled to free himself … this was no fae!

Her thighs tightened like a vice around his hips, the pain making him gasp. There was no possible way he could perform now. The creature's face elongated and hardened, casting aside all illusion of a fae and becoming fully demon. Darian's fear tumbled out of control. This was a demon: a succubus. One that, by forgoing the usual form of a beautiful, seductive woman, meant not to drain his life energy during sex, but to kill him outright.

Long, needle-like fangs dripping a vile green venom grew from now slavering jaws, her tongue emerged, small and pink at first before lengthening, splitting into a thin, forked red protuberance that licked his face and neck.

'Pretty human, have you no loving kiss for Bruxa?'

Her fingernails had become long, curved talons that raked down his body, drawing blood. Using all his strength, Darian fought back, but the succubus was too strong: her desire to play with him before ripping his body to shreds made her determined.

'Tell me,' said Darian, 'I need to know before you kill me. Who summoned you to perform this execution?'

'Pretty boy … such a pretty boy … Bruxa knows you will taste so sweet … As does this …'

The demon popped the lifestone into her mouth and swallowed it. Throwing back her head, she howled in victory, knowing something inside Darian's soul was dying with the loss of the stone. The last fading ember of hope. Her eyes glowed with triumph: now for her reward. She leant down, sucking and licking Darian's neck, taking her time to savour his taste before devouring him – body and soul.

All too aware that he had but seconds to live, Darian made one last, desperate attempt to fight back. As he forced his head away, the tip of one fang pierced his neck, deep enough to drip venom directly into his bloodstream. Not enough to kill him, but enough to give him a brief burst of Bruxa's own strength. He heaved the startled succubus off his chest and thighs, throwing her to the floor.

Without hesitating, Darian sprinted to a full length mirror, smashing it into shards with one well-aimed kick. Then, grabbing the largest piece of jagged glass, he held the makeshift weapon before him.

The room boomed with mocking laughter. 'Pretty boy, you have made so many enemies in this life but you are going to die without ever knowing who sent me to kill you.'

Bruxa, confident in her superior strength and speed, rushed forward and found only air. Darian had sidestepped with his innate agility honed in the backstreet slums of Tehran. Using all his strength, he swung the glass shard in a tight arc, decapitating the succubus in one stroke. Her body crumpled, erupting into a writhing mass of agonised flesh, other forms she had assumed – including the fae – appearing and merging back into the mangled abomination like a half-remembered, monstrous nightmare. With eyes glaring with shock and hatred, the head screamed and screamed … a horrific sound that could curdle even dragon's blood.

'Die you bitch,' Darian muttered as he fought to stay conscious, the venom already surging through his bloodstream like liquid fire.

Instinct screamed that he should flee, find some dark safe place, but his mind fought back, desperate to retrieve the lifestone. Swallowing, Darian approached the now twitching body with the glass shard, preparing to crudely dissect the succubus's carcase to find the stone.

The head stopped screaming and laughed in baleful, mocking triumph, knowing the stone was lost to her assailant. Both parts of the succubus's body collapsed into thousands of squirming slug-like sections that burrowed through the floor and disappeared – taking the lifestone with them.

'Noooo!'

Darian fell to the floor, searching with desperation for the precious lump of enchanted basalt, but it was gone. Too weak to move, in too much despair at the loss of the stone to care, he lay clutching his stomach as the venom fire in his bloodstream intensified and a black shadow passed over his mind and body, sending him into a dark oblivion.

Early morning daylight streamed through the bedroom

… he had been there for at least a day and a night. Shivering with cold, stiff and aching, Darian rose unsteadily to his feet and attempted to leave the room. There was no doubt that the succubus's venom had affected him. He felt different as a human being, changed. Darian's hand went to his chest, felt his heart beating slower, yet his agitated, colder blood seemed to speed through his veins. *Curious.*

He staggered out of the room and down onto the street, seeking a Hansom cab, but the weakness returned and he fell to his knees onto the cobbles.

'Sir, may I offer some assistance?'

A couple of well-meaning passers-by, spotting his confusion and shaky gait, and then his fall, had paused to help him. Darian looked up and, at the sight of his face, the woman screamed and swooned back into her partner's arm. The man hurried her away, muttering, glancing back at Darian with fear in his eyes.

Darian spun around. At every turn people shrunk back in horror at the sight of his face … what in Hades had the demon done to him?

Somehow, he found the strength to pull himself back up the steps and into the house. Once inside he sought out a mirror. He paused at first. What would he see? A monster?

Bracing himself, Darian approached the silvered looking-glass that hung from the wall in the hallway. Though gaunt and marble white from the trauma of the poisoning, his good looks remained.

But none of that mattered. Not with the extraordinary change to his eyes …

THE CHILL

London, 1888

There were no words to describe the depth of John Harbinger's hatred. A soul-deep anger that fuelled his crusade against fraud, greed and the betrayal of the most desperate and emotionally vulnerable. It was that anger that allowed him to brave East London's dangerous and teeming back alleys to seek his prey.

Wey Lane was no different from so many streets in Whitechapel: narrow, cobbled and illuminated by just a sliver of the bright summer daylight that was otherwise shut out by the overhanging and crammed-together warehouses and workshops that lined it. There was no room for carriages, and Harbinger noted a good-quality landau with a matching pair of greys waiting at the entrance of the lane, its driver fending off impudent street urchins with increasingly impatient flicks of his long whip. Harbinger was convinced the landau's passenger would be that night's victim.

He strode down the alley, grateful the appointment time was late morning, when the worst part of the journey was the stench from a nearby tannery and the day's accumulation of filth of the streets had not yet built to intolerable heights. By night the city's predators would rule the shadows, the thieving blaggers and fingersmiths and drunken thugs spoiling to beat up a toff foolish enough to seek out the cheap, tawdry services of the local wagtails or visit their mistresses in their lodgings.

Harbinger had disguised himself. He was wearing the everyday garb of one of London's lower middle classes. Although smart enough, his suit was in a simple brown twill, his waistcoat plain cotton, his bowler well used and scuffed by wear: a far cry from the pure wool and silk attire he usually wore as a wealthy gentleman. He altered his manner too, no longer confident with the upright bearing of an ex-military man but stooped and uncertain, as befitting someone overburdened by hard work and care. He spotted a middle-aged woman, being supported by a maid, and his anger returned. No gentlewoman should be walking in such a low and disreputable area, especially with only a young girl as company.

The women stopped, hesitant, outside a narrow, half-timbered dwelling wedged between two workshops, the house a rare survivor from an earlier era that had somehow avoided demolition as Whitechapel expanded from an outlying village to one of the capital's commercial hubs. The building had not endured by standing out, proud of its antiquity, but by remaining inconspicuous in the lane's many deep shadows, cloaking itself with them and falling into near dereliction.

No lights were showing from inside and Harbinger could see the young maid attempt to dissuade her mistress from entering, but the older woman's pale face, partly hidden by her mourning veil, was determined, her mouth fixed in a grim, thin line. Again supporting her arm, the maid accepted the woman's resolution and helped her up the short flight of steps to the heavy oak front door. As it opened, they were ushered in by an unseen person, so swiftly it was as if the house had swallowed them into its darkened maw.

Allowing a few minutes to pass, Harbinger followed them up the steps and knocked with a deliberate hesitancy on the old door. Again, it was opened quickly, just enough to allow him to enter. Once inside, he took in the oak-panelled small hall lit only by a candle in the hands of an elderly man wearing old fashioned clothes that were clearly of some quality but now stained and fraying at the seams. What was left of this gentleman's white hair was long and pulled into a bow at the nape of his neck. Nearly blind, with a milky film over his once-pale blue eyes, the man extended his hand in greeting towards Harbinger.

'Welcome, my friend, my name is Mr Sageworth, John Sageworth. My dear wife Emma is the one who will help you in your quest for answers.'

Harbinger introduced himself as Bert Cummings and allowed the old man to take his hat and cane as he waited for the inevitable request for money. He did not have to wait long.

'My sincere apologies for this indelicacy, Mr Cummings, but we are old and frail and have to find the means to heat our home and live. Her fee is two guineas.'

Harbinger noted a hardness to the man's wheedling tone as the fee was mentioned and was not fooled by this show of frailty. These people were skilled mountebanks, robbing the grieving without a shred of conscience. Feigning shock, his hands shook as he emptied his purse and fake tears ran unchecked down his cheeks. 'So much. This is all I have …'

The old man snatched up the handful of coins, leaning forward with a whisper of conspiracy: 'That will be fine, Mr Cummings.The fine lady sharing your session has been most generous.'

Ushered into a parlour lit with a single oil lamp, Harbinger recognised the set-up from so many fake séances: a dark room fitted out with many long curtains and wall cabinets; places to hide tricks and illusions. A modern phonograph had pride of place on a lace-covered central table set with six chairs. Clearly business was good to afford such a device. Harbinger sat down, a discreet distance from the lady in deep mourning and her anxious maid. Another knock on the door announced the arrival of more customers. A young couple, white-faced and fearful, well dressed and as out of place in Whitechapel as the lady, they sat down in silence, but the woman clung onto her husband as if her life depended on his stalwart support.

Harbinger did his best to curb his fury. All these people had suffered a recent bereavement. All sought some comfort in proof of the safe delivery into a happy afterlife for their loved ones. They were here to be robbed and duped as so many had been before. Soon the medium would arrive to perform some mock spiritual mumbo jumbo while she played something on the phonograph to attract the spirits. Then the fun and games would begin in earnest. Eerie voices, floating trumpets and, if skilful in illusion, spirit faces and billowing ectoplasm would appear.

At this point, Harbinger would expose the frauds,

pouring light on the photograph of a face dangled on the end of a fishing line, the ectoplasm no more than a length of glowing gauze. There was a price to pay; the distress and disappointment of the deceived, the violent fury of the cheats caught in the act. Pandemonium always followed exposure, with fists flying, usually in his direction. But Harbinger held firm. He had lost his beloved wife as a result of such a visit to a duplicitous medium. Lost not to death but to insanity.

The death of their only daughter at four years old to diphtheria had started the downward spiral for poor Emily. Desperate for comfort, she had gone on her own to a parlour like this somewhere in London where the medium had tormented her with visions of a child lost, alone in the darkness and afraid. Two failed suicide attempts had followed, as his beloved wife had thought to seek her daughter in the afterlife, and Harbinger had been left with no choice but to commit her to the care of a nursing home. Unlike the horrific public asylums, this was a serene, compassionate place of refuge run by gentle nuns. The advantage of his wealth. The only advantage, because all the money in the world could not restore his wife to the lovely, carefree woman he married or bring back their adored little Charlotte.

His sorrowful musings ended as, with all the participants in the séance seated, the medium made her grand entrance in a swirl of black lace and silks. She was a handsome woman, slightly younger than her husband, used to holding the reins of power as she held one imperious hand up, demanding everyone's complete attention. Her voice was equally strong, educated, with a faint trace of a Scottish accent.

'Welcome pilgrims. You wish to voyage with me to the worlds beyond this sad veil of tears to seek your loved ones. There is nothing to fear, they are not lost to you except in body. Now, let us touch hands and create a circle of love and friendship.'

She settled back in her high-backed seat and closed her eyes as her husband dimmed the oil lamp, creating a nervous shiver among all but Harbinger, who had witnessed so many scenes like this. In fact he was bored as well as angered by them. Just for once, he would relish something innovative with the trickery, something that could fool even him for a brief time. Anything but trumpets and the inevitable table-tapping and moving.

The old man addressed the seated guests in a whisper. 'Please, do nothing to disturb or interrupt my beloved Cora now she is entering a state of trance, it will do her great harm. Remain seated whatever happens and do not break the circle of hands.'

Stifling a sigh of impatience, Harbinger's fingers joined with those of the lady's maid – her hands trembling like a captured bird – and then on the other side with those of the bereaved husband. Sageworth turned off the oil lamp, provoking a gasp of fright from the veiled lady, and the room fell to an uneasy silence broken only by nervous breathing and the occasional cough.

The loud moaning began, Cora Sageworth emitted a peculiar and supposedly eerie groan as her mind sought to break through to the afterlife. In fact Harbinger knew it was to disguise the sound of her husband readying the special illusions. He would be an expert in stealth, softly padding around the familiar room in stockinged feet. His wife reached for the phonogram and, winding it up, released a melody currently popular throughout London's pubs and music halls. The incongruous refrain of 'Where Did You Get That Hat?' so jarred with the anxious and expectant atmosphere that Harbinger was forced to bite down hard on his lip to avoid laughing out loud. There would be plenty of time for that later when he recalled the morning's adventure to friends at his club.

Timing was crucial in these exposures. Too soon and nothing was proven, too late and the sitters at the séance would be exposed to too much emotional trauma, the very thing Harbinger was trying to prevent. So he waited, through the farcical moaning, the ridiculous tune and the eerie hush that followed. The maid yelped as a puff of icy air passed her cheek, Harbinger gave her hand a reassuring pat; it was only old Sageworth with a bellows. His wife dropped her head in a dramatic gesture before raising it and announcing she had contacted spirits who wished to show proof of the afterlife and give messages to some of those present.

Harbinger could feel the rising expectation all around him, giving him a sharp twinge of guilt at the prospect of crushing their hopes. But this was fraud, extortion; why should these poor people be duped by the Sageworths and their ilk? True to his expectations, the table began to rock from side to side and rapping could be heard from the walls. To the astonishment to all besides Harbinger, a glowing trumpet appeared to hover above the assembly … yes … they had as little imagination as the other frauds. He prepared to leap to his feet to expose them, but the sound of a child's voice cut through the awestricken silence.

'Mummy, mummy … where are you? It is so dark here and I am scared.'

The young mother gave a little cry. 'That's my

baby, my Johnny …'

Sickened that this had happened so early in the session, Harbinger stood up abruptly, strode across to the window and hauled back the curtain, flooding the room with morning light, dim yet bright enough to show Sageworth dangling the painted trumpet on a long line and a little lad, very much alive, standing by the open door of a high dresser, where he had been hiding until summoned to compound the trickery. Not a street urchin, the child shared the Sageworth looks plus a cruel, pinched face with mocking eyes. A willing accomplice.

'I suggest you return the fee to these good people,' Harbinger thundered. 'Their hearts are broken enough already to suffer from evil frauds like you.'

The séance broke up into confusion and accusations. Throughout all the pandemonium, Cora Sageworth sat unmoving, straight-backed and composed, her basilisk eyes never leaving Harbinger's.

As she prepared to leave, the bereaved lady pulled back her mourning veil to address him. 'Young man, I know you think you have done a good deed this morning. But is crushing the hope of the bereaved such a noble cause?'

She left before he could answer. The young father had Sageworth pinned up against the wall by his scrawny throat and, tempting as it was to let him finish, Harbinger knew he had to intervene.

'Your anger is justified, my friend. But this vile little worm is not worth getting in trouble with the law over.'

'It would be worth it,' snarled the young man, 'but I am all my poor Hester has left now.'

He let go of Sageworth's neck, pushing him to the

ground before gently taking his distraught wife's arm and striding out of the house. Harbinger also began to leave, but as he stepped past the still-seated and eerily-composed medium, she reached out and grabbed his wrist with a surprising speed and strength. Her face set in a sneer of contempt. Her eyes glazed with cold inner fury as Cora Sageworth tightened her bony fingers around the investigator's wrist. He tried to pull away but it was as if he was caught in a vice made from bone and sinew, fuelled by her hatred. She spoke, low, quiet, little more than a whisper, returning to her Glaswegian roots in her accent in her fury.

'Mr Harbinger, you think you are so very clever, don't you? We knew you would be here one day or night. We made the mistake of expecting a learned gentleman, one with the courage to use his own name.'

Harbinger relaxed. There was no point fighting the woman's painful grip, she would have her say and release him soon enough.

'Cora, you disappoint me, surely your spirits could have warned you.'

'Jeer all you like, but you do not have the moral high ground. Not while you ruin the livelihoods of good people who seek nothing but to comfort the bereaved,' she continued, narrowing her eyes as her anger increased.

'Outright lies and shameless trickery at a high cost, you mean,' interrupted Harbinger, sickened by her sanctimonious claptrap. 'That is seen as exploitation and fraud by the rest of society. Cold, calculating, heartless leeches like you deserve to be exposed.'

The medium began to ease her grip on her nemesis, but it was just a ruse. As he relaxed and began to move away, she caught him off balance and hauled him closer to her face. Her eyes widened and bore into his.

'Do what you will, you mocker, you destroyer of hope and serenity. There are forces at work against you now, dark forces beyond your knowledge and control.

'Wrap up warm, Harbinger … as warm as you can. Not that it will help one jot when the chill finds you.'

Harbinger had had more than enough of this claustrophobic dark room and the Sageworths' nonsense. Pulling away with an abrupt tug, far stronger than he would use with any other woman, he pushed past old Sageworth and the malign child and headed for the door, with Cora's triumphal last words chasing him out, 'And it will find you, John Harbinger … It is already on the way …'

Harbinger returned home to his townhouse in Knightsbridge, his humble garb confusing the Hansom cab driver he had hailed, though it was nothing the flash of gold coin could not diffuse. As the narrow carriage passed through sunlit London streets, its passenger shivered, puzzled. Harbinger glanced out of the Hansom's window, expecting to see an advancing rain cloud cover the sun, but the sky was a uniform cerulean, not a cloud to break the endless blue. He dismissed it with a shrug to continue to muse over the morning's unpleasantness.

Once safely within his own home, he set his valet, Browne, the task of organising a plentiful supply of hot water brought up to his bedroom, needing to wash away the stench of corruption and contamination that appeared to have seeped into his skin from that dingy little house. Or more accurately from the odious Sageworths.

Refreshed and once more in clothing more suitable for a gentleman, Harbinger found his soul was still troubled and restless. He decided to take his daily visit to see his wife in her nursing home early, needing to be reminded why he was so determined to walk this dark path. He found her as ever sitting in her favourite chair by an open wide bay window, gazing out at a neat little garden but seeing nothing. Her slender hands held tightly together in her lap as if afraid to let go, her demeanour crushed and hopeless.

Closing the window against a brisk draught, he then kissed Emily's pale forehead and sat down opposite her with a sad sigh. Nothing had changed; her cornflower blue eyes, that once sparkled with so much life, were as dull as ever, deep shadowed and red rimmed from weeping. Prising apart her hands, Harbinger took them in his and began his everyday routine, talking to her as if she was listening and not locked in a place of darkness and perpetual sorrow. He spoke of trivial day-to-day matters, problems with the servants, the latest gossip from her past circle of friends, none of whom would deign to visit her now; anything but their tragedy or his mission.

Gliding silently into the room in that mystical way of nuns, one of the sisters brought Harbinger a tray of tea and biscuits. Her shy, downcast eyes betrayed her admiration for this man and his unswerving love and devotion to his stricken wife. So many of the wealthy patrons of the home had dumped their inconvenient family members here, never to return. Except to attend their funerals, of course Society's standards had to be seen to be maintained. But not Sir John Harbinger, a man of seemingly quiet dignity but with the threat of an inner fire not far beneath the surface. An attractive man, too, tall, of noble bearing with his patrician features, intelligent green eyes and dark hair.

'Any change?'

The same question every day, met with the same sad reply of 'None' from her carers.

'But maybe the poor wee lass just needs more time,' replied the nun in her soft Southern Irish accent. 'One day she will hear you and come back to the light. We pray for that to the Blessed Lady with all our hearts.'

Harbinger thanked the sister, grateful for her faith and genuine optimism, something he could not share, abandoned, like his own belief, since losing both his wife and daughter. As the nun began to take a discreet leave, he raised a hand to ask if a shawl could be brought for Emily.

'I am concerned she will take a chill, Sister Rosario, with this unseasonal nip in the air.'

'My Lord?' The sister looked mystified, checked her patient's temperature by a gentle hand on her forehead. 'I am sorry to contradict you but your wife is perfectly comfortable. In fact I would even suggest letting the window open as it is so warm and stuffy in here.'

Harbinger accepted her diagnosis. It seemed the dark, shadow-filled world of the Sageworths still lingered. Nothing a stiff brandy wouldn't erase.

He waited until he and Emily were alone again, then took her face in both hands and kissed her unresponsive lips. Then he spoke, gazing into the blank eyes while caressing her hair, lank and dowdy now where once her amber tresses had shone as if always lit by sunbeams, even at the dead of night.

'Emily, my treasure, my heart and soul … I love you … I will always love you. I will wait for you to come home to me, even if it takes an eternity.'

Only then did he allow himself to shed a few bottled-up tears. They fell unwanted on his cheeks. Just a few, for he feared a dam-burst if he let his self-control slip for just one moment too many.

Rising from his chair, he kissed her one more time before leaving. Promising her he would return the next day; a vow he never broke, even when confronted by all manner of difficulties such as London shutting down after a blizzard of epic proportions. The memory of his hours of battle on foot through the snowdrifts affected his composure. Though it was early summer and the evening balmy, with a gentle southerly wind, Harbinger shivered and regretted not bringing his cape.

The cold did not leave him on his private carriage ride home, and now he feared the onset of some sickness, something he could not give into, not for his crusade but to keep his promise to Emily.

Back home, he retired to bed early and fell into an uneasy slumber.

Early sunshine flooded his bedroom with a promise of a warm morning but Harbinger awoke feeling stiff and numb with cold. He washed and dressed quickly and asked for one of his park hacks to be saddled and brought to the front door. A brisk ride to Hyde Park and an enjoyable canter down Rotten Row was all he needed to get the circulation going. One of the stable lads brought a dark chestnut mare to the door, knowing she was one of Lord Harbinger's favourites, a swift but steady sort, hunter-bred, by the name of Rosie, who was unafraid of London's teeming traffic and noisy crowds.

As her rider approached, the mare threw up her head, eyes rolling, her ears laid flat back in extreme equine alarm. She backed away sharply along the cobbled drive, dragging the unfortunate groom still valiantly gripping the reins. Hearing Harbinger's familiar, soothing voice, she appeared to calm down, but as he stepped closer, the mare reared, striking out with her front hooves as if defending herself from some ferocious predator. But her fear was not of her master; her attention was clearly fixed at some point behind him. Harbinger turned to seek the cause of her uncharacteristic terror but there was nothing there. He called out to his staff to search the grounds. Perhaps some nerr-do-well was lurking in the ornamental bushes?

His men searched. But no scoundrels were found.

He ordered her groom to take Rosie back to the stable block. 'Bring out old Samson. I'd like to see how he behaves.'

Never skittish, the elderly pony had belonged to his wife, her beloved childhood pet, which until her pregnancy and illness had still carried her safely around the Park on gentle hacks out. Harbinger's heart twisted in grief as unbidden memories crowded into his mind. His beloved daughter Charlotte had started riding the pony too, just before her death. Harbinger himself had been teaching her, not trusting the precious life of his daughter to a groom. He wiped away the inevitable tears clouding his vision.

As soon as the snow-white Welsh pony approached the front of the house, the animal's demeanour changed. Eyes bulging, he snorted in alarm, baulking and shying, refusing to take another step forward. Fearing for the old boy's health, Harbinger had him taken back. He was unwilling to force Samson closer to whatever was spooking the pony. This little chap had been much loved by his wife and daughter; he would not risk his life over an experiment.

Harbinger returned to his house. Refusing to be put off by the curious behaviour of the two most sensible horses in his stable yard, he changed out of his riding clothes and reappeared dressed for a brisk walk. A stroll into the heart of Knightsbridge to enjoy catching up with the news and the fine coffee served at Bullers would do the same job as his abandoned ride in the Park. He set off at a brisk pace but repeatedly stopped to turn around. The sensation of someone close by was too strong to be ignored, but as at the house, there was no-one there.

But the cold had not abated. Around him, well-dressed fellows wore smart linen blazers, their ladies carried delicate parasols to protect them from the now hot sun, but Harbinger walked enveloped in his own personal Ice Age, his lips blue with cold, his fingers clenched in pain, despite him blowing on them as if on a frosty January morning. At Bullers, he craved a blazing hearth, but of course no fires had been made up. So he huddled, shivering in a back corner away from the wide open doors and windows, drinking three boiling hot glasses of black coffee in succession, to no avail. His invisible companion was there too. He noticed baffled customers stepping around an empty area of the shop floor near his chair, aware of something there but unable to ascertain what. His only slight comfort was that, like the horses, people were not afraid of him.

He had already concluded his peculiar affliction

was the onset of some malady, most likely a serious influenza. But this horrible sensation of being followed by an unnatural entity, compounded by the unease of others, made for a more far-fetched and unwanted conclusion.

Once home, he ordered his puzzled staff to make up fires in the drawing room and his bedroom and, pouring himself a triple measure of cognac, made himself as comfortable as he could before the blazing hearth. At one point, his concerned valet asked if he could call Harbinger's physician. Something the master of the house readily dismissed. After two hours with no sign of the warmth from the fire reaching his chilled bones, Harbinger finally agreed and let Browne send a footman to fetch the doctor.

Within the hour, Dr Grainger had made a full examination of his client and, after taking his time washing his hands while he contemplated his diagnosis, joined Harbinger in the fiercely hot drawing room. The heat from the heavily-banked hearth was unbearable; the night air outside was still warm from the pleasant day. Entering the room was like stepping into an inferno, yet his patient still complained of being cold.

'Lord Harbinger, you have me at a complete loss. My examination has found no sign of any ailment or malady that could explain your condition. By all diagnosis, you are in perfect health.'

The doctor shook his head. 'In fact, I wish all my patients had your strong constitution, My days would be filled with leisure and not concern.'

'And poverty,' Harbinger noted, managing to find a wry smile. 'With no fees, your occupation would not yield many pleasurable pursuits. You need us sick ones.'

'Only you are not sick, my Lord,' Grainger replied with a sigh as he prepared to leave. 'At least not by my knowledge of ailments. There is no doubt you are unnaturally cold. I can feel your hands; they are like blocks of ice. But all your bodily functions are normal; everything is working as it should. I can find no physical or mental explanation.'

That the physician had found no illness of the mind was a great relief to Harbinger; that would be too cruel after what had happened to his wife.

'Then what is causing this?' he demanded. He was angry with himself for raising his voice to this good man, but the constant cold was worsening and bringing with it a growing despair. 'Shall I seek a second opinion?'

The doctor gave Harbinger's shoulder a firm squeeze of concern and support. 'Indeed, yes you should. But not from the field of modern medicine. I think you should seek the answer in the dubious, dark circles you insist on dealing with.'

Pausing at the doorway, Grainger turned back to his aristocratic patient. 'As both your physician and a friend, John ... I would suggest you seek a more unorthodox solution with utmost haste.'

Once the doctor had left, Harbinger got as close to the hearth as he could, but none of the heat from the blazing logs reached his skin let alone seeped into his frozen body. He felt delirious, on the verge of insanity, with the bizarre impulse to climb into the fire, to let the flames bathe him and drive the cold from his bones. Fortunately Harbinger had enough self-discipline and strength of character to fight the suicidal impulse and he sat back heavily into his chair, celebrating his victory over the crazed urge by emptying a full balloon of brandy. But the liquor trickled down like a taste-free river of ice instead of the aromatic flow of the normally throat-warming amber liquor.

Harbinger's growing depression was pushed to one side as awareness dawned of a change in his surroundings. No-one had entered the room but he was not alone. Leaping to his feet in fury, the aristocrat paced the drawing room, hauling aside the heavy brocade curtains, opening cupboard and sideboard drawers – even small ones – remembering that baleful brat of the Sageworths. Despite a lifetime of staunch scepticism, he was not surprised to finish his frantic search empty-handed. Harbinger stood still, held his breath and waited.

He could not hear any movement or breathing but the frigid air that first seemed to surround him had now coalesced into a singular point about six feet to the left of him. Not solid, yet still an entity of frozen hatred that glared with hidden eyes straight into Harbinger's soul.

He stood his ground and stared back into seemingly empty space. It made no sound, and did not attempt any communication, but Harbinger knew it was there. If this was a bold statement of its existence, of its intent to haunt and harry its victim into madness and suicide, it had picked the wrong victim. Gathering up his strength of character and willpower and focusing on creating a shield of indifference, Harbinger ignored the malign presence and strode toward his private office, the one room in his household that only he could unlock and enter. He lit an oil lamp, illuminating an unassuming small room containing little more than a crowded bookshelf and a wide oak table piled high with books and documents. This was his war room, the private place where he planned his forays into the world of fraudsters and cheats.

As he expected, he was not alone. The presence reappeared behind him, a shimmering intensity of unearthly cold, but again he ignored it. Until it spoke or attacked him, he would continue to disregard it, an action he hoped would cause the ice being some considerable vexation. Perhaps enough for it to leave him in peace. What point was there in haunting someone who was unafraid?

Harbinger soon found the letter he sought, sent by a noblewoman, the widow of one of his cousins. Lady Jemima Petersley was convinced a medium she had recently contacted was genuine. Indeed her faith in the man was enough to stake her erstwhile spotless reputation on. Jemima was not a fanciful woman, or one given to infatuations or obsessions. Knowing of Harbinger's mission, she had been motivated by curiosity alone to seek audience with the medium, not a need to speak to her late husband; a man she was already convinced was safely at peace and enjoying his rest in Heaven after a long battle with a painful illness that had given him time to settle his affairs and reassure his wife that she was loved.

Investigating this particular medium had not been a priority for Harbinger as the man did not charge a penny for his séances. Compared to the Sageworths he was almost harmless. But not completely; he still spun delusion and lies to the bereaved. Harbinger had no plan of action, no means to defeat his invisible foe. Grasping at straws was not his style, yet if there was a chance, however slim, that Jemima's medium did have some supernatural knowledge, he concluded it was worth a visit. He had nothing to lose and everything to gain.

He spent the rest of the night intending to be fully awake in the drawing room, sitting as close to the blazing hearth as he dared. Harbinger was not sure what evil the glacial entity was capable of. Was it a mythical ghoul, for example, a creature that could suck the soul from a living body? He had to be prepared for any attack – even he did not know how to defend himself against a spirit foe.

The man's address in Camden was within a long walk from Harbinger's home, a convenience he was grateful for. The risk from the entity frightening his carriage horses, causing them to bolt out of control through London's crowded streets, bringing mayhem and risk to life and limb, was too considerable to ignore. Harbinger set off at a brisk pace but, as he anticipated, he was not alone. The baleful glare of the creature bore into his back like rods of frozen iron creating a new hindrance – raw, physical pain, no doubt to wear down his resolve. It would not work. Harbinger carried a deeply embedded bullet in his hip bone from the Afghan war and though it could be agonising at times, he never let it rule his demeanour or life. Nor would this.

Harbinger's search for a certain Edward Baker brought him to Mornington Crescent, once a gracious Regency terrace built in a tranquil rural setting, now engulfed by the ever-growing sprawl of the capital and become a working class area. The Crescent itself had a reputation for housing many of London's artistic and bohemian types and it seemed Mr Baker had found a sympathetic refuge here. His home was in the main early development, one that had yet to be divided into multiple residencies. Clearly the medium was not short of available funds.

A knock with a well-polished brass door knocker brought a homely, middle-aged maid to the door. Harbinger requested a meeting with her master but the woman's face twisted with genuine anguish.

'I am sorry to refuse you admittance, my lord, but Mr Baker is most poorly and should not be disturbed.'

Shivering with the unexpected cold, she glanced over Harbinger's shoulder, alarmed by the unseen presence.

'If it pleases you, sir, leave your card and Mr Baker will send word when he is well enough to receive visitors again.'

The sad and resigned tone of her voice suggested this recovery would be unlikely. Harbinger was able to see into the gracious Regency hallway, still decorated with the original duck egg blue and gold silk wall hangings ... a gracious residence for a scoundrel.

'Let Lord Harbinger in, if you please, Rosie. I have been expecting him.'

Ignoring the maid's loud sigh of disapproval, Harbinger stepped past her to confront a slender young man, his blond hair long and unkempt from sweat. Despite the time of day, he was dressed for bed in a night shirt, over which he wore a dark blue velvet smoking jacket. He stood on weak and unsteady limbs, supporting himself by two sturdy canes.

'Show our honoured guest into the Chinese parlour. The fire is well stacked and merry in there.'

How did this man know about Harbinger's affliction of constant cold? His curiosity now fully roused, Harbinger followed the maid into a bright, pleasant room decorated in the Chinoiserie style of an earlier time and fashion. His baleful unseen tormentor had not entered the house, adding to Harbinger's intrigue. He sat in an elegant, high-backed chair close to the hearth and studied the medium closely as he walked with a painful slowness to join his visitor by the fire.

A male medium was less usual but not unheard of in their close-knit and jealous society. He was far younger than the usual trickster, a man in his early twenties, remarkable only for his ordinary appearance. It was only on closer examination that all was clearly not right with the medium. His extreme pallor suggested serious illness, and when he coughed into a kerchief with the wracking, painful wheeze of consumption, the white linen was stained with bright, fresh blood.

'Forgive my rudeness but I will not shake your hand in greeting. As you can see, Lord Harbinger, I am closer to the Other Side than to this world.'

'I am sorry to see you in this state,' Harbinger replied with sincerity; this vile scourge of a disease was no respecter of age or class.

'Something people will not have to endure for long.' The young man attempted a smile but the gesture appeared to tire him and trigger another fit of coughing. He poured a foul-smelling concoction into a glass, the viscous liquid staining it to the colour of dried blood. He drank it all down, grimacing, for it clearly tasted as bad as it looked, but it appeared to quieten the cough and raise the man's demeanour. An opiate no doubt. No cure but at least a source of comfort to a dying man.

'Knowing you were on the way, I put a strong bane

on my house, forbidding the Chill from entering and giving you some respite.'

Harbinger's mind span, already off kilter since the arrival of the inexplicable freezing entity. He started a barrage of demands and questions, but the medium stayed his outburst with a weary gesture.

'Sir, you have already included me as a target in your list of charlatans to publicly humiliate and expose, so any explanation will be in vain. You also dismiss the existence of the spirit dimension as spurious nonsense. Yet you are here and you are not alone.'

Harbinger did not answer. This young man had him at a disadvantage.

'So, shall we put aside our differences and assume you would appreciate some help,' Baker continued with a wan smile of conciliation. The maid entered the room with a tray of refreshments set for one. Harbinger accepted a bone china cup of Indian tea and waited until she had left the room before answering.

'Agreed. And I apologise. My hostility has been founded on reality.'

'But your reality has taken a considerable blow, has it not, Lord Harbinger?' replied the medium before succumbing to another spasm of violent coughing. Harbinger waited until the young man had recovered from the attack, averting his eyes from Baker's distress for the sake of the consumptive's frayed dignity. The coughing fit was a bad one; Harbinger could not avoid the site of an alarming flood of red blood and dense, darker clots drenching the young man's clothes.

'Excuse me,' Baker somehow managed to gasp between the coughing. 'I must change my attire.'

He returned within a few minutes in an identical but clean jacket, his face less gaunt and pained. A more relaxed Baker sat back in his chair and gestured to his guest to continue.

'So Mr Baker, what exactly is this thing? And how do I defeat it?'

The medium took his time before answering, as if struggling to find terms that Harbinger would understand and accept. One so sceptical would not accept mystical and esoteric terminology. His voice sounded stronger as he leant forward to address Harbinger.

'The Sageworths are indeed complete frauds and extortionists but they are well connected with the secretive world of occult practitioners. Many of these are highly dangerous people, human fiends no man would willingly cross.'

Baker waited until those words were assimilated before continuing, 'The Sageworths have colluded with others that you have exposed and together have summoned a Chill. A minor but deeply unpleasant demon. Not very bright but ruthless and vindictive and unstoppable …'

'Yet you prevented it entering your home,' Harbinger interrupted.

'If you would allow me to finish, sir. Unstoppable by any mortal human of this realm. As I said, I am far closer to the Other Side. One small advantage of being a dying man.

'You are a good man, Lord Harbinger,' he continued, 'one who has experienced tragic loss, and your mission is well-intentioned. Protecting the grieving from scoundrels is a noble cause. You do not deserve this cruel torment.'

To his surprise, Harbinger's heart went out to the suffering medium. Maybe Jemima's view on Baker was closer to the truth. That even if deluded, this man was sincere. Yet asking him for help defeating the Chill seemed a step too far.

A woman's piercing scream echoed through the house. Harbinger leapt to his feet. The cry appeared to come from a downstairs room. Had the Chill breached Baker's protection? He ran to the source to find Rosie the maid stood distraught by Baker's bedside. And Baker himself, whom he had left in the Chinese parlour, was lying there in bed. His wasted body was slumped to one side, a pool of life blood soaking his chest. Harbinger stood there in shock, his heart hammering as he realised that years of carefully-layered scepticism and disbelief had been disproved.

Despite his shock, some part of him knew he should stay to aid and comfort the maid, but this was too much to take in. He ran from the house and into bright daylight and, with no care who saw, doubled up and retched behind a privet hedge. Was he going insane or had he really spent minutes in conversation with a ghost? His legs still shaking and weak, he began to walk away. Soon he was uncomfortable, far too hot in his thick woollen overcoat, scarf and gloves. Removing them, he raised his face to the sun, and its warmth caressed his face.

He was also alone. No sense of the entity encroached on his life. Passers-by showed no puzzlement or alarm, nor did any carriage horse spook as it trotted past him. Unbelievable! Baker had done it. When he had passed on to an afterlife he had defeated the Chill. Though Harbinger was still badly shaken, common decency and deep gratitude forced him to return to the medium's home and do all he could to assist the distraught maid. When briefly alone, he grasped Baker's rapidly cooling hand, muttering a sincere thank you to a dead man. Something that no longer seemed bizarre as it would have done but a mere hour before.

To the delight of his household, Harbinger returned in better spirits, with no call for a fire to be made up. Thanks to the medium, his life had returned to normal. At least, part of his life. Nothing could be pleasant and enjoyable while his wife languished in her lost land, an exile from the world and all who loved her. And no-one could love her as much as he.

Harbinger's arrival at the nursing home was normally a quiet affair. He would be let in by a discreet nun and pass through the quiet corridors in silence. But not that evening. An elderly nun opened the door, and her serene features broke into a broad smile of delight at seeing him. In a joyful fluster, she ushered the aristocratic visitor in, clapping her hands in excitement.

'Lord Harbinger, it is a miracle! All our prayers have been answered.'

He ran past the nun, heading straight to his wife's usual favoured place by the window. He found his beloved Emily sitting quietly reading a book, and when she looked up and saw him approach, her face lit up with delight and love. He held her in a tight embrace he never wanted to end. Had the power of his love and the faith in prayer of the nuns wrought this miracle?

Emily gently touched his face and gazed up into Harbinger's eyes, now flowing with tears of joy. Exultant tears he did not mind sharing with the world.

'I was so lost, my love, lost alone in silence and darkness,' Emily spoke with some hesitancy after so long in silence, 'but then an angel approached me, lighting up my darkness. He came to me with our Charlotte holding his hand and with that beautiful, sweet smile of hers.'

As Emily grasped his hands, her face seemed to glow with an inner light, one soft and serene and stripped of all distress.

'It was Charlotte, most definitely her, John. She had never been lost and alone when she passed over. She tried to tell me but I was too deep in my grief to hear her.'

Harbinger listened quietly. The old suspicion and cynicism had not left him completely but the day's events had deeply shaken the foundations of his belief. How could he not try to be open to what Emily was telling him? And even if there was doubt, would not life be better for both bereaved parents to have hope?

Emily continued, 'They told me to walk out of the bad place, that I did not belong there. That a wonderful home together awaits us all, but only when we are summoned to the light.'

'An angel?' he managed to mumble, 'with golden wings?'

His wife shook her head with a little laugh. 'No, John, he was nothing like the holy pictures. Just a gentle young man with long fair hair and blue eyes, yet he seemed to be made of light and compassion. He said he was called Edward and he told me you must carry on your mission … but only with his help. My dearest, can you fathom such an extraordinary thing?'

Harbinger nodded though his tears. He could.

Now.

DANIEL AND LYDIA

Yorkshire, 1855

One of the coach's rear wheels caught in a deep rut, tipping its passengers to one side. Lydia fell against her guardian's shoulder, a stolid, satin clad wall of flesh scented with no nonsense carbolic soap. A body as unyielding as Aunt Maude's character. Lydia mumbled an apology, which was met with a curt grunt of disapproval, and returned to her half-hearted study of the passing late spring landscape. The sight of villages set in pretty wooded valleys and well-kept fields and pasture had long since lost its novelty value. Each mile put her past, happy life behind her and brought her closer to an uncertain future among strangers.

Two changes of horses earlier, Lydia Carrew had left her family home in Greenwich to make this journey. The mansion where she had spent a carefree, cherished childhood was now an empty shell. The laughter and love had drained away, remaining only as memories and a few precious mementoes locked in a small wooden chest that she clutched tightly on her lap. Her aunt had tried to wrest it off her at the start of their travels, wanting to put it with the rest of their luggage above the coach. Always an obedient and respectful young woman, Lydia had resisted with uncharacteristic ferocity. The box contained all she had left of the memories of love and happiness.

In the end Maude had relented, unwilling to create a spectacle and without a single notion as to why this plain little box meant so much to her charge. Lydia was a girl of 16, on the edge of womanhood, who had lost her family in a recent boating accident on the crowded Thames and was now alone in the world. Maude wasn't even a close blood relative but a very distant cousin of Lydia's grandmother. But common decency and society's mores insisted someone respectable had to escort Lydia to her new home, and Maude was the only family member living in London. The gold sovereigns in recompense certainly eased the burden. At least Lydia was a quiet girl and not some frivolous chit simpering with foolish gossip. That would have been unendurable.

Maude considered Lydia's pale features pallid and her dark hair plain. Her large grey eyes were too child-like, more suitable to a doll than a young woman, and her figure too slender to be womanly and attractive as a potential wife and mother. But none of this was her problem. Once she had delivered her charge to Wychaven House, she would never need to see her again.

Lydia must have dozed off, her senses dulled by the quiet, rural landscape and hypnotised by the rhythmic whirr of the turning carriage wheels and two-time beat of the trotting horses. She awoke from a dreamless slumber with a start as the carriage lurched and turned up a gravel drive. Wide, gracious and sweeping, the path was not towards a coaching inn, so this had to be her destination.

What was to be her new home, she discovered, was a Palladian-style country house of considerable substance. Her relations were clearly far from penniless and their hospitality not based on greed for her inheritance. Perhaps this change in her life would not be so worrying after all. Lydia's spirits lowered again as she looked out of the window at a formal but dense, tangled woodland growing to the edge of the drive. It looked unkempt and uncared for, as was the drive itself, where tall weeds poked through the gravel. Her former fears returned. Ownership of such a palatial home was no guarantee of wealth.

Movement caught her eye; a young man strode through the woods, a lanky gazehound loping at his heels. He looked across to her carriage, raised one hand in greeting and smiled. Lydia, as a well-bred young lady, did not respond. Though the man was attractive and well dressed, he was still a stranger, his rank in society as yet unknown. Her brief glance did make her wonder about the man's pallor, an unhealthy white with deep shadowed eyes. Lydia sighed sadly; consumption was no respecter of the lives of the young.

Lydia forgot the brief encounter at her arrival at the house. As the carriage pulled up at an impressive main entrance, an elderly servant in dusty, faded livery creaked down the stone steps and opened her door. Lydia could hear her aunt's sniff of disapproval. Any plans she had to stay for a few days at the house now dissipated at the lack of servants and dilapidated state of the estate.

'I will take my leave of you here, my child,' Maude simpered in a weak attempt at pleasantry. 'You will be well cared for here with your family. I have a long journey home and much business to attend to back in London.'

Lydia accepted her aunt's brief, moist kiss of farewell on her cheek and alighted from the carriage. The coachmen unloaded her few valises, leaving them on the ground before climbing back on board and setting the horses back into a trot down the drive. Lydia watched the carriage depart with a wistful tear. Her aunt had engendered no affection in her heart but had represented all that was left of her old life, the London she had known and loved.

The elderly servant was clearly too frail to carry her bags anywhere, so Lydia picked up two of the lightest and did her best to negotiate the climb up the steps.

'I'll get the boy to bring up the rest, miss,' the old man muttered with a tug of a non-existent forelock.

Lydia wondered briefly if the young man she had seen in the woods was the 'boy' as she stepped into the main entrance hall. The interior was as grand as the house's classical exterior, with many large marble statues of ancient Greek gods and goddesses and a vast 18th Century painted landscape of the house positioned in pride of place above the first flight of sweeping mahogany stairs.

Her first impression was of grandeur, the second of emptiness and cold. Not a dread supernatural chill but the cold from a draughty, empty building that had not seen the benefit of lit fires for some time. She turned to the elderly servant for some explanation.

'Her ladyship sends her apologies but has taken to her bed with a vexation. She requested you spend the day in the warmth of the drawing room. It will take some time for your quarters to be aired and heated up.'

'Is there no-one else dwelling in this big house?'

A brief flicker of unease darkened the old man's rheumy eyes before he shook his head.

'No, miss. Apart from the lad who cares for the carriage and ponies and his mother Mrs Grady, who is the cook.'

'No maidservants for her ladyship? No grounds men?'

The old man beckoned towards a corridor leading from the hall. 'This way, miss. The drawing room is ready for you. I will bring some afternoon tea presently. This is a quiet household these days. Lady Anne prefers it.'

At least the lack of staff explained the neglect of house and grounds; an estate this big demanded an army of servants. Lydia followed the man into a comfortable room and the welcoming warmth of a blazing hearth. Before she sat down, she wandered around the room and found it spotless, with no dust on the knick knacks and family portraits on the shelves and mantelpiece. Maybe the lady of the house was just being sensible, living only with what she needed.

Lydia took off her cloak and settled by the fire. Within minutes the butler brought in a silver tray of tea and little cakes and left them before her without speaking. With no-one watching, ravenous and thirsty from her journey, Lydia devoured the fare with unladylike haste and rapidly downed several cups of tea. Exhausted, full and now warm, she fell into a heavy slumber.

Someone gave her shoulder a firm squeeze, another hand caressed her hair. Lydia awoke with an abrupt gasp of surprise, but there was no-one else in the room. She breathed in deeply as if to stop her fearful racing heart. It was nothing but a waking dream. What else could it be? Any further thoughts were lost as the door opened and the lady of the house swept in on a rustling wave of black taffeta and lace. Lydia began to rise from her nest of cushions but she was stopped by a curt, raised hand.

'Remain seated, my child.' Lady Anne's voice was quiet, world-weary but not unkind. 'You have had a long journey and must still be fatigued.'

She sat down next to the younger woman as the butler took away the tea tray. 'And there is no need for formalities. We are family. Nearly all there is left of a once happy and prosperous tribe.'

Lydia took her relation's hand, little more than fragile, bird-like bone with a papery covering of thin skin. This house was not haunted but it seemed Lady Anne was. Preoccupied by the past and the losses that still tormented her, she spent her declining years in unending grief.

'But you, my dear girl, may be a gift to this troubled family. New life, new hope. Maybe you and your future children will bring this old house back, filling it once again with colour and laughter.'

Exhausted by her journey and the constant drain of her own sorrow, Lydia was grateful not to be pressed into conversation, but shown to her room by the old lady herself. Candlelight brightened a simple, recently cleaned and well-aired bedroom of a comfortable size for a single occupant of status. It was furnished with the least threadbare curtains and coverings, the bed linen brand new, startling white against the faded fine wools and silks. Muted hues of what were once bright blue, green and gold. Her aunt's lips touched Lydia's cheek, a kiss little more than a cold, dry whisper, and the young woman was left alone for the first night of her new life.

Once ready for bed, Lydia blew out a candle on a cabinet beside the four-poster and was grateful for the new linen's fresh, clean smell above the overall fustiness of the coverings and the room. The bed had not been heated by a warming pan but the cold sheets meant nothing compared to her fatigue. She succumbed straight away to a deep, dreamless sleep, the first in many months. One so deep, she did not hear a key turn from the outside, locking her in the bedroom.

She slept undisturbed until just before dawn. The darkness had not yet lifted, but a few eager birds had begun their chorus as if impatient for the light about to breach the horizon. She heard the snuffling, inquisitive sound of a dog passing beneath her window and, safe within the house, allowed her curiosity to prevail. Wrapping a shawl around her shoulders, Lydia peered from behind the old brocade curtains to see the same young man she had glimpsed on her arrival at Wychaven. To her relief, he did not look up and catch her looking but paced the path surrounding the house with the loyal dog at his side. At first Lydia was puzzled by the old-fashioned nature of his garb, a mode long gone in London. She chided herself for such petty disapproval. This was a long way from the capital; why should country folk be subject to such folly and whims?

The man was soon lost from view and Lydia returned to her bed. Shortage of servants had taken its toll, she reasoned, as she drifted back into sleep. Why else would this man work such very long hours for the mistress of the house? Soon she was again asleep, but this time haunted by unpleasant dreams, of running in terror through dark woods and the howling of a great, fierce dog.

She shook off the fast-fading memories of her nightmares on awaking to a drab, wet morning. Rain beat against the bedroom window, driven by peevish gusts as if impatient to usher away the last days of summer. Lydia began to weep openly, tired of maintaining decorum at all times. She was all but alone in this bleak, loveless mausoleum, with the sad company of the elderly mistress of the house. The loss of her parents had never felt so raw, so piercing as in this first morning of her new life. It was only after her crying had left her red-eyed and weary from the burden of sorrow that she noticed a fire had been lit in the hearth while she slept and a tray of cold meats, fruit and thin slices of bread left on the sideboard for her breakfast.

Lydia pulled herself together, angered by the presumption. As there appeared to be only male servants in this lonely house, it was obvious that one of them had been inappropriate and entered her room unannounced. It may have been only to make the fire and bring the repast, but it was still wrong. She decided to insist on hiring her own lady's maid, using some of her inheritance money. Anything else would be unseemly. As she sat by the table and ate the simple fare, washed down with some plain water, Lydia noticed a letter on the tray. It was a note from her aunt with instructions.

My dear child,

I am unfortunately indisposed today and cannot keep you company at breakfast. Please avail yourself of the library and music room. Wilson will take care of your needs. Explore the house if you will but most of the rooms are no longer used and are locked.

Aunt Anne.

Still fatigued by the previous day's journey, Lydia took her time getting up, returning to bed for another couple of hours. No-one disturbed her to collect the tray from the meagre breakfast or to help her dress for the day. She realised she would need some preoccupations to survive living in this house, empty of so much beyond dusty memories. Back home she had enjoyed the chaperoned company of her young friends on trips to museum exhibits, the theatre or just the fun of their chatter and laughter over high tea at each other's homes.

All those bright, happy memories were fading fast. She already missed the servants that shared her past life; the young maids with their giggling stories of dalliance with cheeky footmen and grooms; the gossip from the streets. Her mind wandered to memories of the warm heart of the house. The kitchen, where she would sneak down as a child and get a hug, a glass of fresh milk and a still-warm biscuit, newly baked by the cook, Mrs Barton. Her father had kept a happy household, just and fair, treating the staff as an extended part of the family. As she would one day, when she came of age and could run a household of her own … back in London.

Eventually, she tired of her own company and the impersonal room and, once dressed, ventured out to a house that echoed with emptiness. There was no sign of Wilson or the yet unseen 'boy'. With most of the house shut down, there was little to explore. There were not even any family portraits on the walls for her to look at: curious in a house with such a long history. Nor were there any objects on display that might have had a family connection, some past history behind them. No sign of much-loved heirlooms collected over time that would have given the house a personal and unique touch, leaving an unsettling sterility. It was as if everything from Wychaven's past had been eradicated with a deliberate and efficient precision.

Lydia soon discovered the library. Clearly she was expected to spend the day there, for the hearth had been lit and well stocked and oil lamps spread some scant cheer from the gloom of the rain-drenched day. She scanned the rows of leather-bound books but all were old and as dust dry as their subject matters. Sighing, Lydia searched for a family bible, eager to learn where she came from, learn more of the history of the family whose bloodlines she shared, but there was none. Again a curiosity and further proof there had been considerable effort to wipe out the past. No family existed without a few black sheep in the lineage, but what had happened to remove everyone from Wychaven's past?

A brave attempt at sunlight broke through the daylong grey. Lydia returned to her bedroom and changed into her outside apparel and boots, intending to take a tour of the grounds and outbuildings. Her mind wandered to the young man she had seen twice now. Maybe he could enlighten her on the house's missing history. Villager, servant ... what did that matter? He was another human being, someone to talk to.

Again, there was no sign of Wilson downstairs or any homely wafts of the night's dinner cooking. Luncheon and afternoon tea had been non-existent and Lydia's stomach rumbled in complaint. Walking to the main door, she tried to turn the large brass handles but could not move them. Surely they would not be locked during the afternoon? She tried again and again until her face flushed with exertion, but the door was definitely locked. Anxiety rising, Lydia sought out another exit from the house, walking at first down ill-lit corridors before breaking into a run ... straight into Wilson, who appeared in front of her like an apparition. Stifling a shriek of alarm, Lydia composed herself to demand an explanation of the locked front doors.

'Miss, my apologies, but I am following your aunt's strict orders. The dark encloses this house early this time of year. It would not be safe for a young lady to wander outside unaccompanied.'

'What possible dangers should I fear?' Lydia demanded, unimpressed. 'Do not tell me the woods around Wychaven are infested with wolves or tribes of brigands?'

Wilson bowed, and spoke in a quiet yet curiously threatening tone.

'Indeed they are not, miss. Not for many long centuries. But there are dangers here that a well-bred young lady from the capital would not understand or recognise until too late. You are to stay indoors. At my mistress's command.'

He gave no further explanation of his curious and

cryptic remark. With no choice but to cede to the butler, Lydia walked away from the door, angry and concerned. Was she to be a prisoner in this mausoleum? She looked forward to her next meeting with her aunt. If Lydia was to remain at Wychaven, there would need to be some serious and immediate changes.

Lydia returned to her room and, opening the top drawer of her dresser, expected to find writing material; notepaper, ink and pens. But there was nothing there but the desiccated remains of a dead moth. What sort of household was this? Her anxiety grew and she feared for her sanity if she remained here for long. No company, nothing to do, no nearby town. Despite its size, Wychaven felt claustrophobic, a cage of empty halls and locked rooms. After a while, hunger drove her back down the stairs. Wilson had not answered the summoning bell and Lydia wondered if it was even connected to the servants' quarters.

It was late afternoon, and the return of low clouds and heavy rain created an early twilight, forcing her to light the oil lamp to safely negotiate the dark corridors and steep stairs as she headed for the kitchens. In grand houses like this, the family would stay well clear of the staff and their areas. Any interference caused discontent and embarrassment on both sides. But this was a house with no formally-structured staff hierarchy; in fact Lydia began to wonder if it had any staff at all beyond the elderly Wilson. A theory that appeared to be confirmed when she walked into the main kitchen area. What should have been a bustling, busy scene of kitchen maids preparing food under the stern gaze of the head cook, with steaming pans on the ranges and the tantalising aromas of food, was in fact a cold, empty place. No hams and dried herbs hung from the overhead racks, no aroma of recently baked bread. It was as if no-one living existed in Wychaven. A nonsense of course. There was nothing spectral about her aunt or the elderly retainer. And what of the yet-unseen cook Mrs Grady and her son who supposedly cared for the ponies? What kind of cook allowed her kitchen to remain in this sorry state?

Lydia wandered around, noting the accumulated dust on worktops and on the overhead racks of pans. One small area was left clean and used but devoid of any preparation for the day's menu. She found a kettle and a teapot but the range was unlit and the hoped-for comfort of a cup of tea dissolved into her growing anxiety about the austerity of life in this desolate old house.

'And what do you think you are doing here, young lady?'

Startled, Lydia dropped the kettle as a sharp female voice echoed across the kitchen, the metallic clang seeming so loud. She turned to address her challenger, a rake-thin woman with a flushed face and chapped, work-worn hands. Beside her was a sullen youth, equally wiry. The elusive Mrs Grady and her boy. The woman strode across the kitchen and threw down a large wicker basket onto the work surface next to Lydia. She was bristling with disapproval; a manner that Lydia found most inappropriate for a servant.

'The family keeps to their rooms and leaves us to ours. That is how we like it at Wychaven. Can't speak for you city folk and your modern ways.'

Lydia stepped away. She had never encountered such rudeness from staff. 'I have been left unattended all day, Mrs Grady. Kindly bring a tray of hot tea and some food to the drawing room. I am certain your strapping son can make up a fire in there.'

'All that is Wilson's duties,' sniffed the affronted

cook. 'I've brought a good meat pie, baked this afternoon, for your dinner tonight.'

'Wilson does not respond when I ring for him,' countered Lydia, puzzling as to why the cook prepared meals elsewhere. Yet another mystery. 'That is why I was forced to seek sustenance down here.'

Lydia noticed the colour drain from the woman's ruddy face; her manner became curiously agitated and fearful. 'He is an old man, maybe he has become unwell. I'll send young Grady to seek him out.'

As the lad shuffled away with a surly groan, clearly displeased with his task, Lydia realised she had sounded haughty and unreasonable, and her manner softened. 'I do apologise, Mrs Grady. Of course the poor man could be indisposed, that was thoughtless of me.'

The cook sighed and gave the ghost of a conciliatory smile. 'No need, miss. This must seem a rum set up for a lady like yourself. Truth is, no one from the village will ever go near this house and I only come here to bring food when her ladyship has guests. And never after dark. Wilson manages when there is just the old mistress of the house to look after.'

She took Lydia's arm, lowering her voice to a nervous whisper. 'Come away with me, my child, while you can. The villagers will happily shelter you until we can get you back safely to London.'

Puzzled and alarmed, Lydia stepped back and shook her head, though deep inside, part of her screamed to be heard, desperate to flee with the Gradys from this unhappy, lonely life at Wychaven. 'Thank you, but I have nowhere else to go and no money until I reach 21. I have no choice but to stay.'

Mrs Grady shook her head in reluctant acceptance but added, 'You will want to come away with me soon.

Just do not leave it until too late.'

The sound of approaching footsteps shut down any further conversation. Lydia walked away disappointed not to have learned more. Why did the locals fear the house? And who was the pale-faced young man she had seen in the grounds? As she left the kitchen she met Wilson and the lad in the corridor. The butler looked even frailer and older than the day before, supporting himself with one hand on Grady's thin shoulder.

'Clearly you are ill, Wilson,' Lydia addressed him in a gentle tone. 'I will take advantage of Mrs Grady's delicious meat pie tonight and tomorrow morning will find lodgings close by until I can find alternative accommodation. Clearly Wychaven is not able to support another member of the family at the moment.'

She turned to the lad. 'Be so kind to bring a pony and trap to the front of the house by nine a.m.'

'There is no need for that,' Wilson interrupted with a curt growl. 'This unfortunate situation will soon be remedied. Her ladyship has today been interviewing staff for the house. You will soon have your own maids and the kitchen will be fully functioning again.'

He dismissed the young man with a brisk, impatient gesture, but as Grady left, Lydia could see the boy catch her gaze. No longer sullen, his eyes were pleading and he mouthed the word 'no' while Wilson's back was turned. What was he trying to tell her? Why were they so afraid for her staying in this house?

Mrs Grady made up a tray with a light meal of meat pie and salad from her wicker basket and brewed a welcome pot of tea and, carrying the tray herself, Lydia retreated to her room to eat and think over her curious first full day at Wychaven. As the last wan illumination of true twilight died, she was drawn to the bedroom window by the sound of a horse walking on the gravel path beneath. Once again, the young man appeared, this time riding a handsome black thoroughbred, clearly not the mount of a villager or gypsy. His ever-loyal dog loped alongside. And once again, the man was dressed in the garb of an earlier time, a heavy, caped navy blue coat, a tricorn hat with a blue plume, long brown leather boots that reached above his knees. He glanced around as if wary of being seen and this time, acknowledging her in the window, lifted his hat and bowed to her with polite formality.

To Lydia's surprise, he was far younger than she remembered from the past brief sightings; barely older than her. His pale face was now wreathed in anxiety. With an urgent gesture, he signalled her to open the bedroom window, but she remembered the warnings of danger in Wychaven's grounds and backed away, pulling the curtains shut. Lydia sat on her bed and waited until she heard the sound of the horse speeding away in a brisk canter. Her relief was tempered with a curious disappointment ... with herself. Like the cook and her son, her visitor appeared concerned for her. Why had she been such a silly little fool and not listened to what he had to say? He seemed a well-bred young gentleman with a kindly aspect and, for goodness sake, what harm could he do from the back of a horse so far below her?

The next morning, the brightness of the sun sent warm rays through every gap in the bedroom curtains and Lydia awoke to a beautiful spring day. For the first time, the burgeoning beauty of the estate revealed itself from the gloom. There were pussy willow blooms like flocks of fluffy yellow chicks, banks of daffodils and primroses adorning the edges of the driveway. She could see drifts of pale pink wild cherry and white blackthorn blossom revealed amongst the still-bare branches of the surrounding woodland. Nature's first welcome heralds of better times to come. Her mood was further lightened by a discreet knock at the door. Dressing quickly, Lydia found a breakfast tray outside her bedroom. Hot buttered toast beneath a candle-powered warmer, delicious preserves and a pot of freshly-brewed tea. There was even a small, crystal glass vase with a posy of delicate narcissi on the tray.

Perhaps her fears had been premature, and though her aunt and Wilson were set in their ways, they meant for her to live happily in this empty, sad house, to bring it back to life. That still did not explain the curious manner of the Gradys. Or the brief sightings of her mysterious visitor. Once her breakfast and morning preparations were finished, Lydia went downstairs, disappointed to see that the sunlight had not reached the stairway or hall, which were still clad in depressing gloom. The house needed re-appointing; a large window was needed to bring the blessing of light into the lower rooms. Something she would insist on, once gaining her inheritance.

How quickly had her thoughts strayed to thinking about a future at Wychaven, when the night before had seen her restless with plans of escape. She had planned to seek out the families of her companions in London and plead for sanctuary. It all seemed so overwrought and melodramatic now.

Lydia found her aunt in the drawing room again. It seemed to be the only lit and warm place downstairs, now she knew the kitchen was not in full use.

'Sit by me, my dear, and help me peruse the

credentials of your future staff. It is important to pick the best suited to this remote location and also amenable in character to you.'

The old woman seemed less sad that morning, the glitter of animation in her grey eyes. Lydia obeyed, though close proximity to the old woman was made uncomfortable by her use of overpowering lavender cologne. The morning passed quickly with so many applicants to choose from, but speculating on the house having young people to talk to gave Lydia hope for a better life. Their business concluded amicably with letters of acceptance written to two ladies' maids, a fulltime cook, three kitchen staff and a young footman to help Wilson. Lydia gave a wistful sigh at the beautiful spring morning beyond Wychaven's gloom-laden walls. She decided it was time to speak out against her virtual imprisonment the day before.

'Aunt, yesterday Wilson prevented me from leaving the house, which I found most distressing. He mentioned it was too dangerous. I find this notion hard to reconcile with the fact we are living in England and not the troubled Balkans.'

The amiable expression on her aunt's face hardened. A cold glint turned her eyes to a shade of granite. 'Those were my instructions. Do not blame Wilson.'

Blanching at the sudden change, Lydia chose to continue. 'You cannot expect me to live confined to this house, Aunt Anne, especially on such a beautiful day.'

Her aunt rose to her feet and proceeded to leave the drawing room. At the door, she paused. 'My instructions remain unchanged. Believe me, this is for your own protection. When the new servants arrive, I can arrange for you to have a daily walk with a maid and guarded by the footman. Until then, I insist you remain within the safety of the house.'

'Protection from what ... or from whom, Aunt?' Lydia persisted. 'That young man walking in the grounds?'

All colour disappeared from the older woman's face. She reached out to a nearby chair for support as she swayed in a near faint. Lydia rushed to help her but was rebuffed by an icy glare. 'You have too much imagination, my child. Perhaps from reading too many unsuitable books. You are fortunate that there is nothing of that nature in Wychaven's library.'

'There is nothing at all, Aunt. That is the problem. I have nothing to do or anyone to speak to.'

'Ungrateful chit!'

The harshness in the woman's tone startled and silenced Lydia, who watched with horror as her aunt walked to the hearth and held the letters over the flames.

'Despite not having the means to pay for these people to indulge your every spoilt whim, I have sold family jewellery to hire them. Jewellery that would have been yours on my death. I was fool to think that would satisfy you.'

Chastised, Lydia sank back in her chair. 'I am sorry Aunt Anne. That was indeed impertinent of me. Please, there is no need to hire all those people. Just a maid to keep me company would suffice.'

The older woman appeared to be mollified by her words and returned to her seat. 'Yes, you must have a maid, for the sake of decency. And we need a good cook at residence in the house. I have taken advantage of Mrs Grady's goodwill for too long.'

Unwilling to let the subject of her virtual imprisonment remain unresolved, Lydia decided to press home her complaint. 'Aunt. Unless you can give me some plausible explanation, I must still insist on access to fresh air. What harm could possibly befall me on a quiet stroll around the gardens?'

Lydia had cornered the old woman into a disadvantage, for whatever the perceived danger was, she was clearly unwilling to divulge it, adding to Lydia's suspicions.

'Leave the matter with me,' she finally relented with an impatient sigh. 'I will make some accommodation for the morning, if the morning is a fair one.'

As expected, dawn brought a fair morning, with a welcome warm breeze to cheer the spirit. Lydia's winter had been long and sorrowful and she welcomed any sign of spring and hope. When she opened her bedroom door to take in her breakfast tray, she discovered a blue velvet riding habit left folded beside it. There was also a pair of well-worn velvet boots; lace-up ones appearing too dainty for their purpose. Delighted at this sign of her aunt's acquiescence, she laid the habit out on her bed to get a better look. It was old, the velvet worn and faded in places, and in the same curiously old-fashioned style as worn by her mysterious visitor. It was petite, made for a child or a slim young woman as herself, and Lydia dressed with a sense of rising excitement. At last she was getting out of this dull house and being given a chance to explore her surroundings in her favourite way, on horseback.

She fought back a dam-burst of tears as her mind filled with memories of bright, brisk mornings riding around Hyde Park on Cherry, her neat little chestnut hack, her father at her side on a smart bay hunter. Such happy days, all gone. And where was her horse now? In her grief-dazed confusion after the loss of her parents, so many matters had been taken over by the family's solicitors. Had the mare been sold? Was she being cared for somewhere until Lydia could take her back? She was determined to find out.

Dressed in the habit, Lydia descended into the main hall, her footsteps echoing in the constant silence. Wilson awaited her, holding out to her a matching black-veiled, blue velvet hat extravagantly trimmed with blue ostrich plumes and riding whip.

'Has my horse been delivered from London?'

Her optimistic request was met with a frown and silence from the elderly servant and he gestured for her to follow him to the front door. Outside, Lydia discovered the Grady lad holding the old bay pony who pulled the trap, this time wearing an ancient side-saddle, the sort with none of the modern safety features demanded by the contemporary equestrienne. The tapestry-covered saddle with its three pommels was designed for ladies to take only quiet walks on docile equines. All Lydia's hopes of an exciting gallop across the parkland dissolved into more disappointment.

The boy had a tight hold on the dozing pony with a chain and strong leather lead through the bit rings … The meaning was clear, she was to have no control over the direction or pace of the animal.

'This really is not necessary!' An angry Lydia glanced across to Wilson, whose features had set into a mixture of stubbornness and contempt. 'I am an accomplished horsewoman, used to riding to hounds on high-spirited thoroughbreds. I do not need nurse-maiding like this.'

'Her ladyship's strict orders,' Wilson replied. 'If this does not please you, I can have the boy take the pony straight back to the stable yard.'

Lydia's answer was to walk to the stone mounting block and wait until the lad brought the pony over to stand beside it. Once she had worked out how to sit on the old saddle and arrange her skirts, she nodded to him and they set off in a sedate amble away from the house.

'Sorry, Miss Lydia,' Grady mumbled. 'This must be embarrassing for you.'

'Not at all,' she answered. It was not the lad's fault, after all. 'Shall we will make the most of our little excursion?'

Grady nodded and they wandered along the gravel paths, taking a tour of Wychaven's unkempt grounds. Lydia soon adapted to the pony's choppy, slow pace and the restriction of the old saddle. If the pony stumbled and fell, she would be brought down with it, unlike with the modern saddles that allowed a female rider to be thrown clear and not entangled or dragged. Lydia took in her surroundings; the burgeoning signs of spring – busy songbirds flitting through branches with new leaves now coming into bud; a careless, happy riot of small native daffodils and primroses growing through the freshening grass. As they approached the edge of the surrounding woodland, Lydia hoped that later in the spring a softly glowing bluebell carpet would transform the dull treescape into a magical fairyland.

She was no longer the only rider. Seemingly unseen by the lad, the now familiar black thoroughbred strode beside her pony, the young rider raising his curiously archaic tricorn hat in greeting. Inevitably he was accompanied by his loyal dog keeping pace alongside the horses. On closer inspection the animal seemed to be a type of shaggy grey deerhound. Startled Lydia's mind raced. Why hadn't Grady made any sign of noticing these new arrivals? Even the old pony hadn't reacted at the arrival of another equine and the large dog.

'I do not have long, Lydia, so forgive any loss of manners.'

The man's voice was tense with anxiety.

'I don't understand,' Lydia replied, her own anxiety rising. Was the Grady boy being compliant with this assignment or did he genuinely not see the rider?

'One day you will understand, God willing, when you are safe and far away from this accursed place.'

Lydia reined in the pony and gazed at the man from behind the gauzy respectability of her veil. He was, if anything, more pale by daylight, skin almost translucent. Only his brown eyes burned with colour and passion. There was also something strangely familiar about his pleasant features, as if she ought to know him.

'May I at least know your name?'

A sad and uneasy smile briefly lit up his face. 'Only if you never speak it aloud within the walls of Wychaven. My name is Daniel. Daniel Carrew.'

The rumble of carriage wheels against gravel distracted Lydia, and she turned her head in the direction of the sound. A smart Brougham drawn by a pair of matching greys approached Wychaven. When she turned around there was no sign of Daniel. Badly shaken, Lydia focused on Grady, who stood patting the pony's shaggy neck, seemingly oblivious to the mysterious encounter. Remembering his words, she concentrated on the new arrivals.

'Do you know who her ladyship's visitors are?'

'Yes, Miss Lydia … My mother overheard Wilson yesterday. It is someone up from London. From the family firm of solicitors.'

So that was why the old woman had been so compliant over Lydia's request to get out of the house. This farcical outing was to keep her out of the way. Lydia bent forward and unclipped the lead rein from the bit ring and, to the lad's astonishment, she whirled the equally startled pony around and kicked it onto a reluctant canter back to Wychaven. Once its destination became apparent, the old pony kicked up its heels for the first time in many years and accelerated into a brisk gallop. Lydia laughed at its enjoyment as she too loved the sensation of speed and the wind on her face. As she would soon enjoy the disappointment and disapproval on Aunt Anne's austere features.

To spare the Grady lad any punishment for allowing her to ride free, Lydia skirted around to the back of the house and quietly led the pony into the stable yard, removing its saddle and bridle once out of sight in its stall. She then walked to the front of Wychaven and strolled inside, head held high, aiming straight for the parlour where she was certain her aunt would be speaking to Lydia's solicitor.

The old woman blanched and gasped as Lydia strode in, wearing her riding attire in a bold statement. Their visitor looked vaguely familiar; one of many faces Lydia had encountered in those first terrible days, the blur of shock and grief. He stood up as soon as she appeared, his bland features creased in puzzlement.

'Miss Carrew, I was told you were indisposed and not to be disturbed.'

Lydia paused long enough to enjoy the embarrassment flush red on her aunt's face, then allowed her to save face … for now.

'I was indeed, Mr …?'

'Clive Brand, Esquire … at your service …'

'Of course, Mr Brand. I remember you now. As I said, I was very unwell this morning but felt some fresh air and gentle exercise may improve my situation. Which, as you can see, has worked a treat.'

Lydia sat down in an empty chair, savouring the displeasure emanating in waves of repressed fury from her aunt, a feeling soon to change to concern as the solicitor explained the reason for his visit.

'Miss Carrew, it was brought to our attention by your aunt that there has been no provision for your estate should anything untoward befall you … a situation we all of course pray will never occur.'

The man looked uncomfortable, but despite her racing heart, Lydia sat with a serene composure, her face set with a calm look of interest.

'Lady Carrew has requested the estate revert to her, should she survive you.'

A chill spread to Lydia's heart and froze it for several beats. Of course Aunt Anne suggested that. The estate was falling apart. Her aunt could not afford staff and lived a lonely, frugal life totally dependent on the ageing, ailing Wilson. All this would change with the inheritance of a fortune. Once she was out of the way. She fought back the reason-sapping panic, forcing herself to remain calm and in control ,but failed.

'Miss Carrew,' the solicitor said, rising to his feet in concern at Lydia's pale face and trembling hands. 'I fear your talk of recovery was premature. Shall I call for some help?'

She wanted to speak to Brand alone. Even risk insisting he take her back to London in his carriage; a rash act born of desperation for a young woman alone and without a maid as chaperone, but he was in her employee. He might agree, seeing her desperation. The opportunity was lost. With surprising agility for a woman her age, Aunt Anne had risen from her seat and reached Lydia, taking her arm in a tight, painful grip and manoeuvring her toward the door with an alarming strength.

'There is no need, Mr Brand. I can take my great niece up to her room myself. The silly girl was ill advised to ride out when clearly unwell.'

Lydia had no chance to protest and, once they were out of sight of their visitor, her aunt was joined by Wilson, who grabbed her other arm. Protesting loudly at such treatment, Lydia found herself hustled up the stairs and unceremoniously thrown on her bed. The final indignity was the sound of a key turning in the lock. She was locked in. A prisoner. Weeping with fear and helplessness, she could hear nothing of the exchange between her aunt and the visitor, but shortly after her abrupt incarceration there came from outside her window the rattle and rhythmic clatter of Brand's carriage leaving Wychaven.

It was a small but important victory. She had not signed over her inheritance to that cursed woman. The delay had bought her more time. Lydia sat up from her bed and wiped her eyes. This was no time for girlish sobbing. Her intentions were now clear and focused; a life of penury would be far preferable to living in this dreadful place, her life in danger. Was this what Mrs Grady and the mysterious Daniel Carrew were warning her about?

Lydia had to escape and soon. Brand may well return the next day with the will to sign, and any plea or protest she made to him implying she was in grave danger from her aunt would be used as a sign of mental ill-health. The old woman could be given even more control over her affairs. If this happened she was surely doomed. Lydia's mind raced … could she leave that night? With the door locked, her only exit was through the large sash window and a perilous route along a narrow stone coving to an ancient rusty ladder, left behind by the last servants to maintain the house. Strands of ancient ivy had smothered the old iron frame, covering all but a glimpse of the ladder seen through the tough foliage. She had spotted it from the carriage window on her arrival at Wychaven and seen it as a sign of the house's decline. Now she saw it as a God-given gift, her salvation.

So great was her desperation, a fatal fall from the rickety ladder seemed preferable to another moment under her aunt's roof. With the Gradys already left for the day, she was on her own. If only there was a way of contacting Daniel, surely he would aid her escape. Lydia tore off the skirt of her riding habit, leaving on the riding britches beneath. Decorum and modesty had to be sacrificed if she was to succeed in her daring and no doubt foolhardy and doomed plan. She bundled what she could into her reticule; the paltry amount of coin she had arrived with, her mother's wedding ring, her own jewellery. She then stuffed some basic clothing into a tapestry carpet bag. It was too small to take much, but it was light and would make little noise if she threw it to the grass from the window before making her climb. For now, she tucked it under the bed in case her aunt entered her room before the evening.

As she expected, Lydia was left alone for the rest of the day, not even a supper grudgingly brought to her room by the conspirator Wilson. The warm welcome on her arrival had been all a sham; she was not wanted here, only her fortune. Fully clothed, Lydia got into the bed, pulled up the bedclothes and waited until night.

Despite her nerve-shredding excitement at the adventure ahead, she must have dozed off, awakening to darkness and the house as still and quiet as a tomb. Lydia pulled open her curtains to complete darkness. No sign of light seeped from the house into the surrounding grounds. It was time. Pulling on her warm riding coat, she then eased open the sash window, taking her time to prevent any noise. Once the window was fully open, she swung her carpet bag and, with all the force she could muster, managed to throw it onto the soft grass beyond the drive. So far, so good. Without a backward glance, Lydia eased herself onto the wide ledge and concentrated on edging herself along the masonry toward the ivy-bound ladder. Her fingers gripped into gaps in the stonework, inching forward in small, careful steps. The ledge was wide enough for a slim slip of a girl to move along in comparative safety; it was the poor state of the stone work that made it so perilous.

Lumps of masonry crumbled away from beneath her feet, tumbling to the drive in a clatter that made her heart pound in alarm. Surely it was loud enough to awaken Wilson? She had no choice but to put aside her fear and carry on, trying to ignore each falling shard but flinching as each one dropped, her fearful mind amplifying each impact to a deafening crash.

With a gasp of relief, she reached a branch of old, gnarled ivy, holding onto it in a tight grip, yet knowing it would not take her full weight for more than a second or two before tearing from its hold on the wall. All she needed was something to keep her secure as she swung onto the rickety ladder.

Wet with dew, her foot slipped as she stepped onto the first rung, forcing her to cling on in desperation to the yielding ivy. For a few perilous seconds she hung in mid-air before her right foot managed to return to the rung and this time stay firm. There was no sense of security once she was fully on the ladder, no sense that it was attached to the masonry by anything but her need to escape. Forcing aside any possibility of failure, she edged down, doing her best to ignore the ominous swaying and creaks of stressed old metal yielding to her weight.

The last set of rungs were the most corroded. Lydia could not trust them, so she jumped down to the drive, grateful for her dance classes that had strengthened her ankles and improved her balance. It would have been so easy to have turned an ankle, ruining her escape plan with pain and frustration. Making sure her reticule was still slung securely over her arm, she gathered up her carpet bag and ran along the drive. Going into the stable yard to saddle the pony would be too dangerous; the inevitable welcoming whinny from the animal might be enough to alert her enemies.

The ambient light from the stars when not covered by fleeting, scattered clouds gave her little aid as she entered the wooded area beyond the main house. If danger lurked here, she believed it was nothing she could not handle. What else could there be in an English woodland than foxes, badgers and deer?

What point would there be for brigands to lurk in this remote place hardly visited beyond the visit of a local cook and her young son? As if in answer, a vixen crossed in front of her, raised its beautiful, knowing head as if in greeting then disappeared back into the fern and bramble undergrowth.

Though finding it harder to see the path beneath the canopy of trees, Lydia dared not slow her pace. The drive was long, the road to the nearest village longer. She needed to find the Gradys before sunrise. Another shape appeared ahead of her on the track. Another fox? This was too big, grey and shaggy. England had no wolves but still Lydia halted in fear as if triggered from some primal instinct. The beast gave a low wuffle, lowered its head and wagged its tail as it approached her in a lope. She broke into a nervous giggle of relief; it was Daniel's lurcher.

It circled around her, happy to see her yet aloof, refusing to reach her outstretched hand. She looked up to see its owner approach on foot. At last fate had given her a chance, real hope. Daniel, as pale and strangely-dressed as ever, bowed low in a mannerly greeting.

'Cousin Lydia, what madness is this? Alone in these dark woods and dressed as a boy?'

Cousin? That was what he was? Then why was he not master of the heirless Wychaven? Why was he wandering the grounds and never accepted into the house? Was he the danger the old people warned about? Lydia backed away, uncertain now whether he was friend or foe.

'The sanctity of my life is not assured while I dwell beneath my aunt's roof,' she said hesitantly. 'I must get away, start a new life.'

Daniel Carrew sighed. Even in the gloom he could sense her drawing away from him. And why wouldn't she? It was time for explanation, though one that would give her no comfort or ease her justified anxiety.

'Lydia. You have nothing to fear from me. I am indeed your beloved cousin ... though a most distant one. More distant than you could ever know. I can help you get away from Wychaven but no further than the estate's boundaries. Please, I implore you, do not question why.'

But she would, Daniel knew it. This girl, for all her delicate figure and gentle manners, was made of sterner stuff. Something she must have inherited from her mother's side, for no Carrew female would have been so brave. He gestured toward the path away from the house, keeping his distance, and hoped she would walk with him, away from the accursed fiends that held Wychaven in their withered yet steely grasp.

At first she held back but then ran to catch up with him. Her expression was guarded, alert to danger, but at least she was moving away from the house.

Lydia tried to keep pace with the enigmatic young man and his dog, hoping that the blessing of night's dark cloak would hold, for she had no idea how close she was to dawn and the risk of discovery. The driveway seemed endless, but her companion-in-flight paused as a narrow but gravelled path split away to one side. He spoke in his now familiar melancholy tone.

'Dearest cousin. This choice of path must be yours and yours alone. Stay on the main and longer track and you will reach the gates. I am concerned that this will be the end of your flight. Wilson keeps them locked at all times unless he knows some rare visitor is expected. None of the local folk will ever come here other than the Gradys, who are newcomers to the region.'

'And if I chose the other path?' Lydia asked.

The prospect appeared to sadden her companion, but his reply seemed encouraging: 'It is shorter and leads to a gap in the outer wall of the estate, one I alone have knowledge of.'

'Then I have no other choice ...' she said, but the

pain in his eyes made her pause.

'You will not like what you find along that path. Once taken, there can be no return.'

Lydia shivered at his curious statement but was too desperate to be far away from her aunt and her sidekick that she broke away from Daniel and began to follow the narrow path, whatever lay along it. How could she risk being trapped by the main gates, so close to freedom and hope? She turned and saw he had hung back, hesitant and unhappy. Lydia decided to ignore him and carry on. It was darker still here beneath the canopy of trees. There were many evergreen hollies dense enough to block any light, but the crunch of gravel beneath her feet gave her guidance and helped her stay away from the tangled, untamed undergrowth at either side.

After ten minutes of brisk walking, despite avoiding the occasional tree branch low enough to impede her progress, Lydia stumbled into a small clearing. She discovered an area enclosed by a tall and ornate, once black ironwork fence, cankered with rust and overgrown with creeping plant life. Within were a collection of gravestones and a sombre mausoleum of some antiquity. The last resting place of generations of Carrews. A forgotten place, mournful in its degradation. No-one had tended this private graveyard for an old and once-wealthy family for countless decades. Brambles covered the ground with their sharp thorns and entangling, aggressive growth. The stones were stained with the green and grey moulds of decay and neglect. Some had toppled over as if ashamed to stand proud, their angels and cherubs lost in the deep brambles. The central mausoleum, intersected by cracks like poisoned veins and draped with sickly, light-starved ivy stood on its plinth above the devastation, its mourning guardian angel pocked and stained with erosion.

'I did not want you to see this sad place, Lydia.'

Daniel, tears sparkling in his dark eyes, now stood beside her. Had she contemplated the graveyard for that long?

'The main house has been long neglected,' Lydia noted. 'I am not surprised that this has happened to the family's internment.'

'Then we must make haste, away from this place,' Daniel urged, clearly unsettled by being in the graveyard. 'The gap in the fence is close by; there is still time to make your escape.'

Nodding a curt agreement, Lydia moved away from the fence and back onto the gravel track that seemed to peter out beyond the graveyard, becoming little more than an overgrown narrow route of earth and tree roots. Why would it be any different? Once a funeral was over, her ancestors would have returned along the wider path back to Wychaven.

'Not so fast, you stupid little fool!' cried a familiar harsh female voice, breaking the woodland silence. 'Did you really think I wouldn't expect some sort of reckless adventure after Brand's untimely visit?'

Lydia's mind reeled with the impossibility of her aged aunt and the yet more decrepit Wilson stepping into the clearing, blocking her way. This was madness. Where was Daniel and his big hound? Lydia glanced about her, but she was alone save for her enemies, who stood blocking her escape. Even in the darkness, Lydia could see their eyes gleam with malevolence and a foul orange light, demonic and predatory. Their thin-lipped smiles devoid of all emotion beyond triumph.

'There is no-one here to help you, child, no-one

living,' Wilson rasped, grabbing her arms with hands like powerful talons, pinning them to her side. Her aunt reached into her reticule and produced a kerchief, reeking with ether. Lydia's world disappeared into darkness.

No matter how many times a new life started, the being who called herself Anna Denvers-Carrew never lost the thrill of occupying a fresh new body, to feel youthful human blood course through her again. She unlocked a cabinet in her bedroom and brought out the only mirror, one always kept hidden in Wychaven. The fresh and innocent face of Lydia Carrew gazed back at her, a complete transformation except for eyes that remained old and ruthless. She touched the cut and bruised face with hands gashed with bramble and blackthorn barbs. All this would soon heal and she would be perfect.

A slightly older man stood beside her, with the unexceptional features of the solicitor Brand.

'I apologise, Shadrach my love,' Anne Denvers crooned, reaching up to stroke his face. 'I would have found someone more handsome for you but we could not delay the transformation any longer. Wilson's body was falling apart before my eyes.'

She glanced out over the woodland where they had buried the disused bodies in marked and unmourned graves over many centuries. 'Sadly they cannot all be as good looking as Daniel Carrew.'

She turned back to the mirror and practised a youthful, winsome smile, but the corruption of her inhuman soul failed to achieve the impossible. The shell of new flesh could not hide her deep-rooted evil and monstrous nature.

'It is a shame we could not have held on for longer but we have the foolish brat's fortune and a healthy body that can breed our replacements. We will go on.'

A soft rain tumbled though the still-bare branches but did not dampen Lydia, who stood at the edge of the woodland, gazing at the house. She knew she would never feel cold or wet again. Part of her wanted to mourn that the living world was unreal to her now, somewhere she could observe but never touch. Lost to her forever. Only something new had made this loss just about bearable. A strong hand slipped into hers. This she could feel. Daniel's hand was warm and living. He was real to her now, as she was to him.

'Lydia, this may be of little comfort, but you have won. That monster can only continue her accursed existence by inhabiting a body of the Carrew bloodline. You are the last. Her vile existence will soon be finally at an end.'

Turning away from Wychaven, she linked her arm in Daniel's and started to walk. By losing her life, she had found love, and she would not be just one of a long line of victims to the demonic Anne Denvers-Carrew and her familiar. She would wreak a terrible revenge, somehow, some way.

After all, she had an eternity to plan it.

GHOSTLIGHT

London, 1837

She lived on the margins, the border between the last stretch of floodplain grassland and the greedy, ever-expanding sprawl of the city. An old lady who kept her back to the new factories in Homerton and the tight rows of new terraced houses. She preferred to gaze out over the mist-wreathed countryside Watch the dip and soar of birds and serenely observe the change of weather and the seasons.

Those who had always lived in Hackney, still thinking of it as their village, treated her with respect. She lived alone because she had outlived her family, her spouse, even her children. She was kind and wise and did no harm. Newcomers would attempt to mock her, just a crazy woman, an old witch who preferred her run-down wooden hovel, living with her chickens and goats, over a new brick house. No-one knew her real name. She was Mother Marsh to the locals, Mad Meg to the incomers.

Despite her isolation, she was not lonely. The path to her home was well worn with folk coming daily to buy fresh eggs, jugs of creamy goats' milk and honey from her bee hives. She thrived through barter; a bucket of coal or some old but clean wool socks in exchange for her fresh, quality produce was as welcome as currency. By daylight, they were happy to stroll to her once-proud, white-boarded Essex farmhouse, now a barely-inhabitable shell since a fire many decades before. By night, few would risk venturing onto the open land, not with the threat of the River Lea bursting its banks and turning the area back to marshland. People had tried to drain and tame Hackney Marshes for centuries but the river had a wild, capricious soul and liked occasionally to remind humans of its power.

There were other reasons for not venturing out onto the marsh after dark. Reasons people kept to themselves, not wanting to sound like superstition-ridden medieval peasants rather than modern citizens of the 19th Century. There used to be real danger crossing the marshland tracks from footpads and highwaymen in the old days, a time no-one was left alive to talk about. But something older, more primeval, troubled many minds. Tales of wandering lights out in the grassland, of frightful moaning sounds coming from the ground. These tales were kept to hushed whispers … as though speaking them might bring them back to reality. And no-one wanted that.

Stepping from a train, a new arrival to Hackney knew nothing of its history. He was a young man with an ambitious spring in his step, an uncomfortable new suit with a high starched collar that had already cut into his neck, and an air of authority that did not sit well with his age. In his briefcase were plans, details of an important project he was assigned to help initiate. An easy scheme, the success of which would help his fortunes with the Corporation.

With a few hours to kill before meeting with the survey team and the project engineers, Philip Proude decided to seek out the site on his own. Spring had blessed the day with warm sunshine and a flirtatious breeze and, using a map rather than speaking to the lower-class locals, Proude easily found his way to the Marshes.

With only an out-of-date description to go by, all he could see was an area of flat, featureless grassland dotted with a few stands of trees. A flock of ewes, all with lambs, grazed in the field, content with their calm surroundings. Further away, tawny cattle tended their new calves. It was ideal; a peaceful site for a place of rest.

He paused and drew in a deep breath to fill his lungs with fresh country air, but it was tainted with the soot and thick smoke from London's household fires and foundries. To his disgust he also detected a whiff of ordure, not just from the nearby grazing beasts but the output of countless humans, horses, dogs and rats. London was already here, making a claim by stealth on the future of the Marshes.

Proude had been told the area for re-development was uninhabited, but a thin ribbon of wood smoke caught his attention. He strode towards it across the grass, carefully avoiding the small piles of sheep droppings and reeking cow pats. City born and bred, Proude considered the best thing for countryside was a new covering of cement.

He discovered a track leading to what had once been a farmhouse. It was now a charred, debris-strewn ruin, yet one chimney and a few rooms remained, and the place was clearly inhabited: a line of washing danced in the breeze, well-cared-for chickens and goats wandered in what once must have been a garden, and smoke streamed from the chimney.

An old lady carrying a yoke of milk pails emerged from the back of the house. His appearance at her property caused her no alarm and she paused to remove the yoke from her neck and stood upright to greet him. She must have been a beauty once, thought Proude, for she was still handsome, with lined but well-defined features and bright grey-blue eyes that had not lost their sparkle. Her faded clothes were old, much-darned and patched but clean and worn with a pride of bearing. Her attachment to the land must be strong, emotional; why else live in the shell of a ruined farmhouse, remote from the rest of the community? For the first time, Proude's confidence in the easiness of his project wavered. This old woman's home was not shown on his map and was situated right in the centre of the development.

'I can tell from your garb you're not here for milk or eggs,' she remarked with a slight country burr so different from the speech of the Londoners who dwelt within sight of her home. A voice from a long-lost past that knew Hackney as a small village surrounded by countryside. 'So you better come inside and tell me your business.'

Nervous of what he might face within the derelict walls, Proude followed the woman into her dwelling to find it far from squalid. Clearly an inherent pride kept the makeshift kitchen neat and spotless. Copper pans hanging from hooks sparkled in the light and a cracked vase full of freshly-gathered wild flowers sat on a central wooden table. Proude shuddered. Closer inspection highlighted traces of the catastrophic fire that had brought this house to ruin: charred wood on the table legs; twisting and warping on the metal kitchen utensils; and black smoke stains in the corners of the room. Gesturing for Proude to sit at the table, the woman fetched two clean and perfect earthenware mugs and made tea from water boiled on a battered old range.

Raising his mug and thanking the old woman for her hospitality, Proude took a sip of the tea. 'I was told by the Corporation this land was empty, uninhabited.'

She folded her arms, a steely resolution in her shrewd eyes. 'Well, clearly it is not. I own all the pasture up to the stand of mature oaks. And I can prove it. My late husband Abe made sure the deeds were kept safe in the vaults of his bank.'

Proude opened his carpet bag and brought out a large folded map. 'With your permission?'

He spread the map out on the table. The area to be developed was outlined in red ink. 'There are the oaks … you are right! The outer boundary of our scheme is indeed your land. I am sorry to have alarmed you for no good reason.'

Mother Marsh's stern and anxious expression did not change. 'But you *have* alarmed me, young man. I may be old but I am not soft in the head – yet. What manner of development are you people planning? Over the years, I have watched the city creep up on the Marshes, hoped to have gone to my heavenly reward before the last of the fields and trees were lost forever.'

The young man sat back in his chair and smiled. 'Then I am delighted to inform you, ma'am, we have no plans to build houses and factories here. Quite opposite … we want to create a garden.'

Mother Marsh did not relax. If anything she became more suspicious as Proude continued. 'A beautiful serene garden, one of rest for the East End of

London's dear departed. All the city's churchyards are full to capacity, some even overflowing in some most unfortunate and unpleasant incidents. The Corporation is solving this with the construction of a number of large, dignified Gardens of Rest, or cemeteries in common parlance.'

'Not here you don't.'

The woman's unexpected, curt reply stopped Proude in his tracks. Was the old crone superstitious about having to live next to a graveyard?

'If the prospect alarms you, madam, then I am certain the Corporation will buy your land, set you up in a fine new home.'

She stood up, manner abrupt. 'It will not be me who objects to your fancy scheme, young man. It's them … Out there.'

'Them?'

Her expression and lack of answer suggested to Proude that she felt she had said too much. There were more locals living on the marsh? The woman briskly turned and began to clear away the tea cups before walking towards the kitchen door.

'Well, if you will excuse me, the goats cannot milk themselves …'

Confused, Proude thanked her for the tea and returned across the fields to his meeting point with the engineers. The hours in their experienced company passed quickly, and as darkness fell, making all further work impossible, the men took their leave and headed toward their homes in the city. Only Proude remained. The woman had aroused his curiosity, and he was determined to know who she meant by 'them'.

Proude strode across the marsh. Though twilight had given away to the night, he was able to make out the path to the old lady's home by a half moon low in the sky and the distant gleam of an oil lamp in her kitchen. It was not far. A low mist, glowing with moonlight, rose from the night dew, reaching his knees and swirling with each purposeful step. It was beautiful, serene, and Proude felt calmed and safe, if a little weary.

A faint blue/green glowing orb moving through the mist made him pause. Proude's heart skipped a beat at the strangeness of the light, too low, too cold a colour to be from an oil lamp or candle. His pace quickened as another and then another light joined the orb. Why had he thought the farmhouse to be so close? The faster he moved, the further away his destination appeared. As he walked, so his feet felt leaden, as though the ground was pulling at them. Proude cried out in alarm as he saw more lights from all directions heading towards him. This could not be a natural phenomenon. Marsh gas on land that had been drained and tamed? Impossible.

Salvation in the form of the old woman's voice and her waving oil lamp freed his limbs from their peculiar torpor and Proude sprinted the last hundred yards to her home, throwing himself past her and through the door with a whimper of relief. He collapsed into a chair, panting with exertion and fear, while the woman fetched a glass and poured a small measure of unknown liquor, handing it to him with a desultory sigh.

'Didn't nobody warn you about venturing out on the marshes after nightfall? Did you even bother talking to any of the locals?'

Proude drained the glass. It was a cheap brandy that burned the back of his throat but was nonetheless welcome. He shook his head.

'Then you are more of a young fool than you look. Striding across the fields with your maps and plans, with no thought beyond promotion and success.'

She sat down opposite him with her bright, sharp gaze boring into his soul. How did she know about his ambitious hopes and plans?

'This may just be a stretch of grass,' the woman went on, 'too close to the city to be left alone by the likes of corporations and developers, but to us, it is old land, full of secrets. Secrets that want to be left alone.'

Proude started to speak but she held up a hand and interrupted him. 'And don't start telling me it's all just superstitious nonsense. It wasn't me who just ran here as if pursued by the hounds of hell.'

Her voice grew sterner. 'Go back to your Corporation. Tell them this land is not fit for change, be it a graveyard or houses.'

'I doubt if anything I can say will change their minds. East London needs another cemetery.'

The woman gestured to his carpet bag. 'Get out that map of yours and I will tell you what to do.'

Proude felt helpless in her company. She now seemed far more than a remarkable, self-sufficient old woman. She was something else, something more powerful. Maybe he had tapped into some inherited ancestral memory from an ancient time, when the power of the crone, the wise woman of the tribe was held in great awe and respect. He did what she commanded without question.

She closed her eyes, held out both hands and passed them over the map before focusing in and alighting on a specific area. 'There. That is where your Corporation will build their Garden of Rest. Your engineers will have already advised against this place; too much danger of flooding from streams deep beneath the soil.'

224

Proude gazed at the map. 'Abney Park?'

'Yes. It will be very beautiful; a serene garden of remembrance and peace. One that will be treasured for a long time in the future. You will get all the success you crave, if you champion this site.'

The woman gestured to an armchair. 'That is all I can offer in the way of hospitality. I suggest you sleep here tonight and return to your world after dawn.'

Proude did not argue. In truth he was exhausted and did not want to face whatever awaited him in the darkness. Once settled beneath an old but clean patchwork blanket, he fell into a deep and mercifully dreamless sleep.

The woman stood on the threshold of her ruined home as the ghost lights gathered in her courtyard. One by one, they took on the forms of lost souls, the spirits of those who had lost their earthly lives to murderers, ancient warfare or other misfortune. Many had been the victims of past floods, and the earliest ghosts were those who had fallen foul of the marsh when it had been a formidable foe, dragging the unsuspecting into its deadly embrace. She looked out across the crowd, the centuries past of forlorn spectres, and shook her head sadly.

'You should move on, my dears ... move on to your heavenly reward. I have protected this land for you for five centuries now, but I am tiring and getting so old. I don't know how much longer I can stand against the outsiders and their greed.'

One by one, they surrounded her, bathing her in their spectral light, giving her a gift of their energy to renew her strength, her youth. Once again she would live on, maybe fall in love again, re-marry, have children and mourn their loss when she outlived them all. And in return Mother Marsh, who had forgotten her given name, would watch out for and protect the ghost lights and the birds and beasts that belonged to this fragile tract of land.

Proude woke at the first light of dawn and rose stiffly from the old armchair. It was damp, mould-ridden and broken. He had not recalled it being so decrepit the night before. There was no sign of his curious hostess anywhere on the property and as he stumbled outside, even her hens were missing from the yard around the farmhouse. Had the whole encounter been a dream? Troubled, Proude returned to his home and then to his office in the city. He spent the day preparing a thorough and decisive report, pointing out the many problems with developing the Hackney Marshes site and extolling the desirability of Abney Park as a better alternative. He submitted the finished report to his superiors and sat back in his chair with a weary sigh.

He could do no more.

Back home, his mind refused to let go of the mysterious encounter, becoming more dreamlike by the minute now he was back in familiar surroundings. Had he really seen those ghostly forms? How had the engineers and planners not known about the woman and her home so close to their development? Unable to let it rest for fear of his sanity, he decided he had to return to the farmhouse.

Proude was certain he had more than enough daylight left to retrace his steps in safety, but confusion soon forced him to halt in the middle of the open grassland. He couldn't find the well-worn path to the woman's farm, in fact he couldn't find any tracks; even the regular narrow paths of foxes and badgers cutting through the grass eluded him. Completely lost, he was alarmed to see the dusk closing in on him with an indifferent unkindness. The rising moon was no ally either, the light illuminating the same swirling mists that had so frightened him the night before.

As the mist approached with a purposeful roiling menace, Proude ran, blindly, with no direction, tripping over dense clumps of nettle and docks. The mist merely speeded up to match his pace. Tiring, Proude cast frantic glances into the vapours and saw figures forming within: spectral humans of many ages and wearing clothes from many eras. Victims and predators alike, all trapped to haunt the marshes for eternity. Proude ran himself to a standstill of exhaustion, but there was no salvation for him this night. No guiding farmhouse light and shelter. His feet caught a trailing bramble and he took a heavy fall, cracking his skull on a hidden pile of bricks, a left-over from a previous failed attempt at building on the marshes.

His blood leached deep into the soil, enriching it, and his spirit arose and became one with his pursuers. Proude was now trapped forever on the marshes, watching over them, protecting them, and allowing the Mother to continue her ages-old guardianship.

HEART OF BRASS

Lincoln, 1892

At daybreak, Edgar Jonah Burke of Bailgate, Lincoln, watchmaker and self-proclaimed genius in all things clockwork, left his spartan living quarters above the premises and entered his workshop. All was as it should be, as it always was.

Synchronisation and precision. Those were the two essentials that made Burke's life bearable. They gave his life order and purpose and assured his continued sanity. Around him, the rows of clocks, gilded carriage, workmanlike mantel and stalwart long case, ticked and whirred in perfect unison. Laid out like the aftermath of metal carnage, the stripped workings of many mechanisms waited for Burke's thin, strong fingers to reassemble them, bring them back to life with their own unique heartbeats. A rhythm the clock mender would painstakingly adjust to match the others in the shop. There must be harmony at all times. Anything else was chaos, a reflection of the anarchy that lurked so close to the surface of the human condition. And anarchy was something Burke abhorred.

He relished this quiet, reflective time alone with his broken children, the precious early daylight hours before he was forced to earn his living and open the front rooms, the shop that would see the hated trespass of the locals. Their brash, loud talk, their stench, all anathema to the fastidious Burke, a stick-thin, prematurely middle-aged man, as tightly wound as a watch spring. What enraged him the most was the misuse of mechanical devices. The over-wound pocket watch; the rusted wall clock; the mantel cast to the hearth by a clumsy maid. Their pain was his.

Burke pushed aside an errant lock of greying hair from his loupes and concentrated on his latest patient, a pretty pocket watch, a whimsical confection of gold, deep blue enamel with a painted enamel idyllic scene of lovers beneath a blossoming apple tree. An expensive item that had the misfortune to cease working after its owner dropped it in a cup of tea. Earl Grey. Burke could smell the contaminating substance in the watch's movement.

He cradled the stricken watch in his hands as if to comfort it. Closing his eyes, he tried to imagine its past as if it could take him back in time. Burke already knew it was French, 18th Century and an object of high status. A delicately-wrought inscription within suggested it was a love token to a French lady. Burke let his mind wander to the doomed court of Louis XVI, imagining the watch to be a treasured trinket from a secret lover to a pompadoured aristocrat. A duchess perhaps. He could almost smell her delicate perfume, the rustle of her extravagant silk gown. Even sense her growing fear at the mood of the mob at the palace gates. So how did such an exquisite object from such a life end up in the sausage-fingered hands of the vulgar wife of a wealthy local industrialist?

Burke shuddered at the implication and an imaginary shadow of the guillotine. Putting the watch back on his workbench, he broke free of his imaginary journey into the past. He was not usually a fanciful man but certain objects did indeed seem to speak to him. These were the ones he wished he could rescue from their lumpen owners, but he was a businessman, one who needed their revenue to eat and keep his shop warm and lit. Though it would hurt him, the noblewoman's watch would return to its undeserving new keeper.

He spent the next two hours painstakingly cleaning every tiny cog, spring and gear in the movement, polishing the tiny rubies and setting the watch ticking to the same rhythm as everything else in his workshop. Content with his expertise and success, he re-wrapped the watch in silk, put it back in its box and put it aside for collection, half hoping the woman would renege and not bother to reclaim it. Of course no-one would leave behind such a treasure, though he had a box of ordinary clocks and watches remaining unclaimed, his work unpaid for.

Burke finished his cherished private time and, after a frugal breakfast of bread and cheese washed down with weak tea, reluctantly opened the shop.

Midweek, with no market in the city, the morning dragged. The slow march of time beat out by his many clocks and marked by the deep resonance of the nearby Lincoln Cathedral bells, whose hourly ringing was joined by the chimes of Burke's patients. There were no customers, apart from a manservant arriving with a carriage to transport his master's now good-as-new long case clock back home. At least Burke did not have to endure the vice of idleness. He was able to sit at the wide shop counter and work on more prosaic assignments, fixing and improving the timepieces of the good citizens of Lincoln.

The clockmaker became so engrossed in his work that he did not hear the tinkle of the shop's door bell, if it rang at all. He looked up and was most startled to see a young man stood in front the counter. Had Burke been so involved with his work that he had been unaware of footsteps? Brushing aside such worrying concerns, he gazed up at that tall youth to discover an unsettling mystery. Dressed in the well-cut and expensive garb of a wealthy gentleman, the visitor carried a wooden box, no doubt containing something to repair. But what gentlemen did not send a manservant for such a mundane task? Nor was there a waiting carriage or tethered quality-ridden horse outside the shop.

Burke's unease grew as he further scrutinised his customer. The young man wore his straight fall of unusual silver-tinged, pale gold hair in an unfashionable length; and, strangest of all, though he was clearly barely out of his teens, his dark amber eyes reflected a sense of great age and cynicism, bordering on evil.

More fanciful nonsense. Burke grew angry with himself. It wasn't even as if he had fostered such a ridiculous state of mind; he did not read novels or attend the theatre and avoided the excesses of lurid newssheets.

As the young man placed the box in front of him, Burke detected a curious, fleeting aroma of dead, decaying flowers and ashes around his visitor, but all his suspicion, his growing unease was swept away as his curiosity over the contents of the box rose. At a deliberate and tantalising slow rate, the visitor removed layer after layer of protective soft lamb's wool from the box, finally lifting out an object that gleamed and sparkled in the dim daylight of the shop.

Burke gasped in wonder, his eyes growing large at the sight of a magnificent orrery. His hands trembled with an instinctive need to touch the beautiful instrument, a clockwork rendition of the solar system, most likely created in the latter years of the 18th Century. The young man gave a slight yet cruel smile and slowly slid the orrery across the counter and into the possession of the entranced Burke.

The clockmaker's fingers traced every inch of the device, revealing its complex intricacy – which, Burke realised, was far beyond that of similar devices made even in his more enlightened times. What unknown genius had made this? By its appearance it was more than a prosaic scientific instrument delineating the orbit of the planets around the sun; this was a toy, a bauble for a man of incalculable wealth. The entire framework of the device was made of solid, pure gold, while the central orb of the Sun was represented by a spectacular large yellow diamond, precision cut into a sphere that danced sparkling fiery light around the shop as if in defiance of the gloom.

The planets too were symbolised by precious or semi-precious stones, all uncut but highly polished and no less beautiful than the scintillating brilliance of the Sun. Mercury was made from moody grey hematite. Venus was cut from a pale, veined turquoise. The Earth was a separate marvel in itself; a deep blue sapphire wonderfully inlaid with emerald and ice poles of pearl and circled by a shining selenite moon. Mars was a magnificent ruby. The giant planet Jupiter a shining orb of banded yellow and orange citrine; its many moons were semi-precious stones of different hues. Saturn was blue lace agate, its extraordinary rings intricately wrought in bands of shining cut stones of different colours. Burke recognised rainbow and rose quartz among them. And finally, Uranus was a large tiger's eye in rich bands of gold and brown.

There had never been an orrery of such magnificence, opulent yet beautiful, an object of extreme desire and as out of place in a humble clock-menders shop in Lincoln as a winged unicorn. The young man spoke for the first time, his voice low, melodious, with a curious, compelling power. Burke was not a religious man but wondered if he was about to become the victim of a Faustian pact? That maybe this was the Devil incarnate?

The youth took back the orrery from Burke's trembling hands, clearly relishing the clockmaker's distress at having to give back the treasure, and told him: 'A good friend of mine treasures this bauble greatly as my gift to him. Sadly it has become temperamental of late.'

Burke's mind screamed a warning, that this was the moment to stay free of temptation, of some soul-risking pact that this deceptively angelic youth would use to try to lure him to damnation. The clock-mender was not a religious man but attended the Sunday services at the Cathedral with the other traders and artisans of Bailgate as a necessary routine to court respectability. Now the countless fire and brimstone sermons he had snoozed through came back to him as a warning of danger.

His hesitation did not go unnoticed. The visitor's

amber eyes gleamed as he lifted the orrery and wound a well-hidden mechanism in its base. The planets began their miniature orbits around the Sun, their moons tracing their own path around their masters, while from within the base came clockwork music depicting the eternal dance of the spheres. Burke sighed with astonishment and felt a desperate craving to possess the orrery, but as he watched, mesmerised by its beauty, his sensitive need for precision alerted him that something was wrong. The orbits were imprecise, their timing out of kilter. The music too was discordant, its charm marred by an eerie resonance that was uncomfortable to listen to. It was as if all the order of the universe itself was set askew. A nightmare vision in miniature of all the chaos and anarchy Burke feared.

'You can imagine how this has disappointed my friend,' the youth murmured, holding up the orrery in distain as if it were a worthless trinket. 'We were told you were the greatest expert in these matters. Can you put it right?'

Again the last dying remnants of Burke's resolve clamoured to be heard. *Say no. Let the man take the desirable thing away.* It had a dangerous beauty. One too great for a humble man to possess, even if only for a short time. Sensing his hesitation, the customer pulled over the box with one hand and prepared to place the orrery back into it, this time without the protective soft wool.

'I was mistaken. My friend cannot abide imperfection. I will get this broken up for the gold, get the diamond reset in something else.'

A howl of protest rose in Burke's soul, reaching the surface as a pained whimper. He held out both hands in desperate supplication.

'Please, I beg you. There is no need for such a drastic measure. The orrery just needs some time and care. I am certain I can fix it.'

'I am certain that you can,' the youth replied with a chilling smile before loping out with silent footsteps, leaving a faint scent of charred dead flowers in his wake. There had been no talk of payment. Burke considered following him to see where he went, but an inner voice warned him the street would be empty. Badly shaken, the clock-mender closed up the shop early and returned to his latest, most spectacular patient.

His hands caressed what had been the smooth gold base of the orrery, his fingertips tracing a complex etching in the surface. Why had he not noticed that before? He yelped as something sharp in the design pricked a finger and a few drops of bright red blood coursed along the finely-cut ridges to disappear into the mechanism. His many years of great care of all things clockwork saved the orrery from being dropped onto the counter in dismay, but Burke stepped back from it in alarm, nursing his cut finger. How could something so beautiful be demonic? The clockmaker decided this was all nonsense, his occasional lapse into fanciful thinking let out of control by a lack of self-discipline. Boxing up the instrument and locking it into his safe beneath the floorboards, Burke decided to take a constitutional stroll around the town.

Outside his shop window, the early afternoon sun gave a mellow gleam to the city's medieval buildings. The first yellowed leaves of autumn twirled and twisted in a pleasant southerly breeze. Burke removed his oil-stained apron, donned a dark grey frock coat and, retrieving his top hat and cane, strode out into real life and the reassuring surroundings of normality.

The walk appeared to have its desired effect. Nodding politely to acquaintances, Burke strolled around the castle grounds, an open green area of great charm in the centre of the city.

His restored good mood did not last. With each step away from his shop, Burke felt increasingly disorientated and ill at ease. At first he fought against it, telling himself he was simply unused to taking a leisurely walk in the middle of a working day, a disorderly act that went against his principles. Before long though the unsettling feelings were too strong to ignore. He was being called out to, summoned by the golden treasure beneath his floor. It wanted him back, demanded his return. Burke turned on his heel and left the castle grounds, the unpleasant sensation decreasing with every step.

Burke made one backward glance, in the direction of the nearby Lawns, the splendid classic mansion that was in reality an asylum for the unfortunate lunatics of Lincoln. He was one of them now. How easy it would be to force through the orrery's malign spell and throw himself at the mercy of the good doctors at the asylum, to let others care for the worries of the world as he slipped into a laudanum-laced daze. Instead he allowed the lure to bring him back, to tear up the floorboards in a crazed scrabble, with splinters digging into his fingers, spilling more blood onto the orrery, which gratefully received it as before.

He worked well into the night, meticulously removing the movement from the orrery base and using a large magnifying glass to check for obvious flaws that would spare him the need to take the mechanism apart and rebuild it. There was no obvious cause for the instrument's disharmony; Burke could see nothing wrong.

Eventually, faint with exhaustion, Burke secured the orrery jewels in the safe and, climbing the stairs to his bedroom like an old man, fell on top of the bed, still fully clothed.

Burke was awoken by the Cathedral bells sounding three and his own shop echoing the peals. Once the noise faded, Burke tried to return to sleep but his attention was drawn to a loud ticking, out of kilter with that of the rest of his charges. How could this be? The movement of every clock in the shop had been working in complete harmony earlier. Burke tried to ignore the discord. Exhaustion had made his limbs leaden, his eyes painful and dry. But the steady tick, tick, tick refused to allow him peace. He dragged himself off the bed and stumbled down the stairs to his workshop.

Lighting a gas lamp, he walked from clock to clock, his highly-tuned hearing able to detect any sound out of synchronisation with the others. All were working well, exactly as he had tuned them, yet still the infuriating out-of-pace ticking carried on. He finished his inspection of the entire shop front and working area to no avail. A curious compulsion to check the orrery also gave no answer. The mechanism remained on his workbench, under cover and silent. With no possibility of returning to sleep with the noise undiscovered, Burke decided to lose himself in work and continued his efforts to solve the mystery of the broken orrery. At some point the irksome ticking stopped, but the clock-mender was unaware, slumped in a deep sleep across his workbench.

He awoke, small cogs painfully stuck in his cheek, the surface beneath his face damp with saliva. Alerted by loud and instant knocking on the shop door, Burke slouched across the room and opened it a few inches, blinking in the bright, midday sun. His visitor was another Bailgate tradesman, Mr Henry Pugh, a nearby dealer in fine furniture. Beneath his arm was a large parcel, carefully wrapped in brown paper ... another mechanical patient for Burke to tend. Pugh was clearly alarmed by the clock-mender's dishevelled appearance: his hollow eyes, the smell of unwashed flesh and crumpled clothing.

'Sorry, Mr Burke ... you are clearly indisposed. Can I fetch a physician?'

Burke was only dimly aware of the man's concerned words; they sounded so far away, drowned out by the infernal loud ticking so jarring and at odds with all the rest. He opened the door wider, ready to step into the fresh, sun-lit air, allow his neighbour to walk him to the care of a doctor. But the noise grew ever louder and so, mumbling an apology, he slammed the door shut and retreated into the stuffy gloom of his shop.

As he walked back to his workbench, to his slavery in the service of the orrery, the ticking subsided, a reward for obedience. Burke did not pause for the rest of the day, struggling with the seemingly impossible mystery of the faulty mechanism, ignoring all but the most basic of human needs until he retired at night, hungry and exhausted and none the wiser.

The same pattern continued for the next few days until, unable to bear his life a moment longer, weak, dehydrated and starving, Burke decided he no longer cared about enraging the eerie customer and was no longer worried over the fate of the orrery. He just wanted peace from the infernal noise. He stuffed his ears with packing wool, binding them close to his head with string, and began systematically to dismantle the movement of every watch and clock on his premises. This was a move too far for his unknown tormentor. The sound of the infuriating ticking became loud and louder; an insistent angry beat that had to be stopped … had to be, for he knew his sanity, his life were under threat.

Returning to his workbench, he melted down some candlewax and, using the packing wool, forced the hot wax into his ears to seal them up, letting out a high mewl of pain as the sensitive skin burned. Not waiting to discover whether this drastic action had succeeded, Burke rushed from clock to clock, throwing trays of pocket-watches on the floor, his fingers prising open movements and jamming them with brutal force. Anything to stop them working.

Such was his frenzied assault on the once-precious mechanical inhabitants of his shop that the clockmaker ignored his unknown nemesis until he collapsed hours later onto the cold flagstones of his premises, every timepiece stilled. There had never been such a deathly silence, not since his first day of trading as an optimistic, bright-eyed young man some 20 years before. Now a ghostly pale, gaunt and crazed shadow of that man knelt on the flagstones and wept in relief. Never had silence been so welcome after a lifetime measured by the steady beat of dozens of clocks. Burke glanced up at the now reassembled orrery. The gold gleamed with its own inner fire. The Sun-diamond, flashing a cold light, mocked him with its dispassionate beauty.

And he realised it was not broken, never had been. The challenge was cruel, demonic, driving him to desperate measures to change the orrery's cursed skewed nature; its music could not be re-tuned from the infernal to the celestial. It would never change. He had been tricked, but why? He was not a bad man, he attended church every Sunday. So what if he had made a few sly business deals over the years. Didn't everyone?

There was a sound and Burke strained to listen.

Tock.

Tock, tock, tock.

It began again, if it had ever actually stopped. Tock, tock, tock, an echoing sound as if counting his heartbeats. His heartbeats! Burke gave a low groan of realisation, for that had been the sound all along: his own, terrified heart hammering louder as he tried to abandon the orrery, knowing he coveted it too much ever to leave it to an uncertain fate with its unseen owner. As for the owner's identity, Burke was now in no doubt that it was the Devil himself.

Now Burke recalled how, on the first night with the orrery in his care, he had planned to run away with the treasure and start a new life far from Lincoln, living off his substantial savings. Even plotted to kill the eerie customer rather than give it back. That was when the loud ticking had started; the sound of a guilty heart.

He could bear it no longer.

Burke was beyond all past concerns. His beloved patients were silenced; his shop closed; his body weak; his soul damned. Turning his back on the gleaming, cursed treasure, with the last of his strength, he hauled on a rope pulley to open the door to a disused basement. As it lifted, he was assaulted by the smell of damp, stale air and decaying boxes, the odour of abandoned memories. He lit an oil lamp and, pulling together the last tattered remnants of free will and faltering courage, began to descend the stone steps into a realm of shadows and hidden loss. Here he kept several large trunks full of items and clothing from his happy childhood and young adulthood. He had no-one left now from those days and each reminder hurt him too much to contemplate ever unpacking the boxes, yet he had been unable to part with them.

Perhaps the thought of its victim contemplating rebellion enraged the harsh spirit of the orrery, for the furious hammering of Burke's traitorous heart began again, much amplified by the cramped space of the basement and its stone walls.

'Enough!'

His tortured cry echoed dully, unheard. Burke rummaged through the forgotten past, casting aside the stacks of old furniture and ornaments from the long-gone family home until he found what he sought … a long wooden box, almost coffin shaped, the unpainted pine mottled blue and grey with rot. It was locked, the key long lost, but the poor state of the wood presented no barrier to his prising fingers, made strong through desperation. The lid fell apart in his hands and, throwing aside protective hemp packing, Burke pulled out a tangle of brass and copper; the component parts of an automaton. It was a project from his youth, inspired by his love for the Mayor's fair daughter; a gift left unfinished and abandoned when she had spurned his shy and courtly advances and married another.

Ignoring the pale bisque porcelain face of what was to have been an automated fairy playing a lyre, its green glass eyes blank and free from accusation as if resigned to its fate of dereliction, Burke pulled out a lump of beaten metal complete with a large ornate key. A clockwork heart of brass. It was the most complex, intricate mechanism the clockmaker had ever made. Its sophisticated beauty made him briefly forget his torment and sigh with pride and delight. He had the makings of genius once, all swallowed up by a morass of heartbreak and disappointment.

He returned to his workshop, clutching the brass heart tightly to his chest, and sought out a sharp, long carving knife …

Lincolnshire Chronicle 1892
Excerpt from *The Curious History of The Clock Mender of Bailgate*

Alerted by blood-freezing screams, the nearby citizens of Lincoln about their daily business broke down the door to the clock-mender's shop to discover a scene of great horror. Mr Edgar Jonah Burke, the proprietor, was on his knees in a gushing lake of his own blood. Clutched in one hand was a gore-stained knife; the other grasped a ticking clockwork mechanism in the shape of a brass heart. There was a large open wound to his chest. Thanks to the quick action of the good people of Bailgate, the man's life was saved. However his sanity never returned. The unfortunate Burke spent his last days at the newly-built asylum at the Lawns. He spent a month clad in a protective straitjacket to prevent any more attempts at cutting out his own heart to replace it with a clockwork version, with

obvious fatal consequences, before sepsis from
his deep wounds finally claimed his life.

The unfortunate madman often raved about a treasure
of gold and diamonds left behind in his shop, warning it
came from the Devil himself. Many searches were made,
both official and from opportunist rogues, but this
object, a miniature planetarium, was never found. The
wise doctors at the Lawns decreed this was nothing
more than the babbling of a lunatic.

It is said that on quiet nights, visitors and inmates
at the asylum can hear the weeping of a man tormented
by hopelessness, along with the loud and persistent
beating of a human heart.

Tock, tock, tock.

ABOUT THE AUTHOR

Raven Dane is an award-winning fantasy author based in the UK. Her published works include the highly acclaimed *Legacy of the Dark Kind* series of dark fantasy/sci-fi crossover novels *(Blood Tears, Blood Lament* and *Blood Alliance)*.

However, Raven's skills in fiction don't end there. Her comedy fantasy *The Unwise Woman of Fuggis Mire* – a scurrilous spoof of high fantasy clichés – was met with great enthusiasm by the reading public. In more recent years Raven has met with critical acclaim for her steampunk/occult adventures *Cyrus Darian and the Technomicron* and *Cyrus Darian and the Ghastly Horde*.

Cyrus Darian and the Technomicron was the winner of the best novel award at the inaugural Victorian Steampunk Society awards 2012.

Raven also has many short stories published in anthologies including one in *Full Fathom Forty*, a celebration of 40 years of the British Fantasy Society, and the first annual of ghost stories from Spectral Press, called the *13 Ghosts of Christmas*.

Further works include poetry, published in an anthology of pagan verse.

She is currently working on her third Cyrus Darian novel.

22722471R00133

Made in the USA
Charleston, SC
28 September 2013